"Author Jed Power has the . . . touch . . . it doesn't get much better . . ."

—Charlie Stella
Author of *Rough Riders*
and *Shakedown*

". . . Jed Power channels the tough-as-nails prose of Gold Medal greats Peter Rabe and Dan Marlowe."

—Shamus & Derringer
award-winning author
Dave Zeltserman

"Fans of Dennis Lehane will revel in the settings and atmosphere . . . an absorbing read . . . a hard-charging plot . . . Boston nitty-gritty."

—Charles Kelly
Author of *Gunshots In Another Room*
a biography of crime writer Dan Marlowe

Praise for *The Combat Zone*

"Power's work, already cover-to-cover forceful, keeps getting better. Boston has never had a better P. I."

—John Lutz
Edgar & Shamus award-winning
author of *Single White Female*
past president of Mystery Writers of America
& Private Eye Writers of America

Jed Power

THE TREASURE OF HAMPTON BEACH

a Dan Marlowe/Hampton Beach Novel

Dark Jetty Publishing

Published by
Dark Jetty Publishing
4 Essex Center Drive #3906
Peabody, MA 01961

Cover Artist:
Brandon Swann

ISBN 978-0-9971758-6-8

10 9 8 7 6 5 4 3 2 1

Acknowledgements

I would like to thank my wife and first reader, Candy, for her great work, which included typing and extensive critiquing, not to mention her barrelful of patience during very trying circumstances this time around. Also, a big thank you to my writing group friends—Amy Ray and Bonnar Spring—for their outstanding critiques along the way. Double thanks to Amy for an extensive professional-level revision on a pile of papers she helped turn into a manuscript. Again, I would like to thank my editor Louisa Swann for her usual excellent work for the eighth time on the Dan Marlowe/Hampton Beach Series. And very importantly, a shout out of thanks to artist Brandon Swann, who has created another amazing cover for this novel as he has for all my other books.

Chapter 1

IT WAS ALMOST three in the morning, a time I'm usually snoring away, but I'd been awakened by an irritating noise. It wasn't loud, just loud enough to pull me from that twilight sleep I sometimes fall into when I've spent more time than I should have at one of the beach watering holes.

I wasn't going to get up at first. I just lay there, hoping that whatever the hell the noise was would stop. But it didn't. And it was one of those puzzling sounds you can't identify so it drives you crazy.

Sleep at the beach in late September is rarely disturbed. Most of the cottages surrounding my own, on this little section of Hampton Beach called "The Island," were closed for the season. So this noise was not only galling, it was unusual.

I ignored the noise as long as I could before my curiosity got the better of me. I rolled out of bed, threw on jeans, a T-shirt, and sneakers and headed out to see what had ruined my half-sleep. I followed the sound—a mixture of scraping and thumping—between the two cottages that deprived me of an ocean view from my front porch. I rounded the corner of the cottage closest to the ocean . . .

And stopped.

It was a dark night, clouds hiding whatever moon there might have been. I stood on Hampton Beach proper, digging toes in the cool sand. To my right were the outlines of a group of small ocean-front cottages. To my left, at a farther distance, the Atlantic Ocean. The dark water blended in with a just-as-dark sky. I could hear the waves lapping against the shore and smell the salt in the air.

A figure I couldn't see clearly appeared to be digging in the sand not far from where I stood. I watched for almost a minute. See, I'm not the kind of person to butt into someone else's business, especially living at the beach with its live-and-let-live atmosphere. But for some reason, the scene I was looking at raised my curiosity level even more than the initial noise.

"What the hell are you doing?" I finally yelled.

The person startled and ran, stumbling as he did.

I gave chase. I hadn't gone more than a few yards before the ground dropped from under me. I tumbled into a hole about the circumference of a child's wading pool and just as deep. I scrambled to my feet, bounded out of the hole, and continued my pursuit, slowly gaining ground.

I was just about to grab his arm when he suddenly turned and swung the shovel he'd been carrying. I ducked, feeling a cool breeze brush my head as the tool missed its target. I lunged up from a crouch and caught my assailant with a fist that glanced off the side of his jaw. I didn't think it connected hard enough to cause much pain, but to my surprise, the man let out a high-pitched squeal and flew backwards, landing flat on his back in the sand.

I bent to catch my breath, then stepped closer. From what I could see in the dark, he was a small man. A bit of a wimp, too. He whimpered and reached his hand up for my help.

The shovel was off to the side, out of his reach, so I grabbed the man's hand and pulled him to his feet. He didn't weigh much more than a half-full laundry basket.

Just as he stood, the moon slid from behind a cloud, lighting his—no, *her*—face, a woman so young I would have carded her if we'd been at the High Tide Restaurant and Saloon.

She rubbed the side of her face where I'd struck her, but I couldn't see any damage. Her eyes were blue and large. She wore a bandana tied over her head, so I couldn't see much hair, but it was blonde, with just a few tufts peeking out. She only came up to my shoulders and looked thin as a starving teenager. She even dressed like a teenager in jeans and a ratty sweatshirt.

"Are you all right?" I asked, shocked to find that I'd clobbered a woman and more than a little relieved my punch hadn't fully connected.

"No thanks to you." Her voice reminded me of one of the young waitresses I worked with at the High Tide.

"Do you always punch women?" she asked.

"I'm . . . I'm sorry." I waved at the shovel. "When you swung that thing, I . . . I thought you were a man."

She turned a bit and rubbed the sand from her rear. It was a nice rear, accentuated in tight jeans. "You're lucky I didn't hit you. You shouldn't have been chasing a man or a woman. I wasn't doing anything wrong. Besides, what business is it of yours?"

She had me on the defensive now, even though she'd swung first. And she'd run. Why run if she wasn't doing anything wrong?

After a minute's thought, I said, "We've had a lot of break-ins around here during the off season."

"And what do you think I was trying to break into down here on the beach?" she sputtered. "A clam's shell?"

I could feel warmth spreading across my face.

"Why *were* you digging over there?" I asked after an awkward silence.

Now it was her turn to get a little flustered. "Like I said, it's none of your business. Now if you don't mind, I'm leaving . . . that is if you're not planning on punching me again."

I muffled a groan. Last thing I needed was for some woman to tell the cops I slugged her in the jaw. I would gladly have carried the shovel to her car or wherever the hell she was going to prevent that. I needed a stain on my almost-rehabilitated reputation as much as a hit man needs his gun to jam.

When I didn't answer, she picked up her shovel and turned to go. Just then, the beam of a flashlight splayed across both of us.

"Hold it right there."

A figure stood silhouetted on top of a nearby dune. I didn't need night-vision glasses to know we'd been found by one of Hampton's finest.

Whenever the Hampton P.D. got a call concerning nighttime shenanigans on this end of the beach, they'd send a cruiser to a street adjacent to mine. The cruiser would park at the end of the street and the cop would climb up and over the dunes to try and catch the perps—who usually turned out to be a bunch of kids drinking.

As the flashlight bobbed slowly down the dune in our direction, the mysterious digger moved to my side. She was close enough I could see her eyes were as frantic as a lab rat suddenly cut off from an addictive drug.

"You've got to get me out of here."

I just looked at her.

"If you don't, I'll tell the cop you attacked me."

I didn't have to think long about that. I already mentioned that I'd retired my previously damaged reputation, right? At least enough I could walk along Ocean Boulevard without wearing sunglasses 24/7.

There'd been a time I hadn't wanted anyone to see the infamous Dan Marlowe, the man they'd heard so much dirt about. Even more important, I had regained visitation rights with my two kids, and they were occasionally allowed to stay with me in Happy Hampton Beach.

I couldn't risk losing any of that, not after all I'd been through to regain it.

I grabbed the hand of my ditch-digging friend and pulled her at a fast jog back in the direction I'd come. Behind us, I heard shouts of anger, commanding us to stop. I wasn't worried about getting drilled in the back. Like I told you, most mischief on the beach at this time of night was instigated by sloppy drunk teenagers, so a cop would be highly unlikely to shoot.

We ran side by side between the cottages, her small hand in mine. A good distance behind us, I could hear the cop's heavy shoes thumping in the sand.

When we rounded the corner of the cottage just before mine, I pulled her close so she could see my face as I put my index finger up to my lips. We moved quietly up the porch steps of my one-story cottage. I opened the unlocked door, pulled her in after me, and eased the door shut.

I put my finger to my lips again and that's when she came in close and wrapped her arms around me. I could feel the shovel she still held digging into my side. But that wasn't all I felt.

She was trembling.

I wrapped my arms round her and we stood there, neither of us moving. Footsteps echoed outside, then a car stopped somewhere on my street. Probably reinforcements talking to the cop who'd chased us.

Footsteps and voices came from different directions throughout the neighborhood along with the occasional squawk of a police radio. Eventually one of those broadcasts alerted our pursuers to something more dramatic than a teenage drinking party.

Cars pulled off—two, by the sound of it—and headed away down the street, their headlights making eerie shadows on my front room window shades.

She pulled back and looked up into my face. "Are they gone?" she whispered.

I didn't want to peer through the curtains. Not yet. "I think so. You okay?"

"Yeah, but I'd be better if I had a drink. Do you have one?"

I smiled at that—the first smile since I'd been awakened earlier by her incessant digging—and headed toward the kitchen. "You're a very lucky woman. You came to the right place if that's what you want."

"And you're a lucky guy."

The smile left my face. I wasn't sure what she meant but, yes, I was lucky. Very lucky for a change.

I *could* have been seated in the back of one of those cruisers.

Chapter 2

I DIDN'T HAVE any hard liquor or wine. I had beer, though, and plenty of it. The sand digger sat across from me on the couch, sipping a cold Heineken. I'd parked in my easy chair. I wasn't drinking anything. It was too late, even for me. Besides, I still had the remains of a hangover from my earlier overindulgence.

We'd been chatting aimlessly for a half-hour now. I decided to bring the conversation back to something meaningful. "You still haven't told me what you were doing digging on the beach at this hour, Monica."

She'd told me her name was Monica Nichols and that she lived in Charlestown, an old Boston neighborhood. She stared hard at me, as though debating whether to give me an answer or get back to the weather. She reached up and pulled the bandana from her head, ruffling her short, blonde hair. A pink streak ran through what I guess is called a bob style. A very small stud sparkled in her nose.

Attractive in a mildly rough way. She was older than I'd first thought, but still only in her mid-twenties . . . maybe.

"Can I trust you, Mr. Marlowe?" she finally said.

"Remember . . . it's Dan," I said. "And unless you were planting the bodies of children you killed, yes, you can trust me. I saved you from the cops, didn't I?"

She mulled that over for a long second, nodded slightly and smiled. "You did." She rubbed her forehead with one hand. "I was looking for something, Mr . . . ahh, Dan."

I chuckled. "That much I figured out myself. What was so important you had to go digging in the sand after dark?"

She looked hesitant again. "I have no one else I can trust . . ."

I gave her my most sincere smile.

"Gold!" she said, her voice cracking on the last word. "A lot of it, too. I've got a map. Well, not really a map. Directions, I guess you'd call them. I've been down here other nights looking . . . But . . . I'm lost. I don't know where to dig. I don't know where to look. I only know . . . I don't want someone else to find it first."

I didn't ask who she meant; she was too distraught. I wanted to give her a minute to calm down. She twisted her hands together, looking around. Seemed she might burst into tears any minute.

She certainly didn't resemble the person on the beach who almost knocked my block off with a shovel.

I leaned forward in my chair, hands clasped and forearms on my knees. "Slow down . . . slow down . . . take it easy."

Nut or not, the word 'gold' followed by 'a lot of it' got my attention. In my precarious financial condition, I couldn't write off any possibilities for monetary improvement that might come my way.

"You're telling me you're looking for gold on Hampton Beach?"

She drew in a deep breath, let it out slowly, and seemed to calm down a bit. "Yes. Fifteen thousand dollars' worth."

That curbed my enthusiasm. Fifteen grand is nothing to sneeze at, but it certainly isn't life-changing, especially if there are two people to consider. I still had two kids to support—as I often reminded myself—and my share of bills. Was there some way I could help with her search and get a little slice of her golden pie?

"How do you know there's gold here?"

I'd been coming to the beach my entire life, and except for some old tales of pirate treasure on the Isle of Shoals twelve miles out, I'd never heard any stories of gold in this area. Being the bartender and tiny-minority stakeholder at the High Tide—the most popular watering hole on the beach—I would have heard about errant pots of gold.

She seemed more relaxed as she took another sip of her beer. "My grandfather told me."

"Your grandfather?" My excitement slipped again. I visualized some old man telling his grandchild fanciful pirate stories while she sat on his knee. Still, I had to ask. "How does he know about it?"

"He put it there."

I sat back, surprised. "What was he doing with gold and why did he put it here?"

She proceeded to tell me a story, the little she knew at least. A story you could've made a movie about—Prohibition, 1930, rumrunners, smugglers, gangsters, crooked cops, and yes, Hampton Beach.

There were a lot of holes in her story, but I didn't interrupt. I listened to what she told me happened over sixty years ago, maybe feet from where we sat.

When she was finished, she stared into my face.

"You want another beer?" I asked. Whether she did or not, I was getting one for myself. This tale had made me forget about hangovers and work in the morning.

"Yes," she called as I headed for the kitchen. I returned with two cold beers, handed her one and retook my seat.

"Your grandfather told you all this?" I asked. Before she could answer, I added, "And how do you know it's true?"

She took a sip of her beer, and I noticed her full lips. Taking the bottle from her mouth, she said, "He didn't tell me all of it. Some I gathered from family stories. Some from my mother. She's dead now, but she told me a lot about Gramps. Not about the gold. I don't know if she knew about that. If she did, she never mentioned it. They never got along. He was already in prison when she was born. I guess my grandmother used to bad-mouth him all the time. I don't think my mother was ever allowed to visit him in prison. But I did, once I got old enough, anyway."

"So your grandfather told you about the gold?"

"Yes. Like I told you, Gramps was a bootlegger for some gangsters during Prohibition. I guess they were smuggling liquor into Hampton Beach from boats. Anyway, there was a shootout, and a cop was killed. Gramps was arrested and sent to prison for life." She hesitated and her eyes filled.

She sipped her beer before continuing. "Almost for life. About a year ago they gave him a compassionate discharge." She grunted and her tone turned angry. "Some compassion. He was in his nineties and dying of a half-dozen diseases. His mind wasn't too good, either. Anyway, I was all he had. I'd visited him since my teens. When he got out, I took him in.

A nurse came a couple of times a week. He lived with us for about six months before he died."

"Us?"

"My son, Sam, and me. He's eight now." She looked at me and added, "My husband died years ago in a car accident."

"Sorry," I said lamely.

"Thanks. So you see, it's just me and my son. We're struggling. We could use that money. We've got almost nothing. When Gramps told me about the gold I—"

"What exactly did he tell you?"

"You have to remember, Gramps was old and sick and his mind was . . . well, you know. But over the course of a few weeks, he managed to tell me about the gold. Every time he'd tell me something that made any sense, I'd jot it down. The same time he got arrested for shooting the cop was when the gold was buried in the sand exactly—he kept saying that word, 'exactly'—a hundred feet from the front door of the Seaview where he was staying with the other smugglers, I guess."

"What else?" I asked, curious now.

She looked frustrated. "I don't know, Dan. He described this area of the beach. He said the gold is buried one hundred feet from the front door of the Seaview. Beside the piles."

"What piles?"

"I don't know. Just 'piles.'"

I was losing my patience. "A pile of what? Rocks? Sand? What?"

She glared at me. "I don't know. I only know the name of the cottage it's buried in front of. The Seaview."

My mind flipped through the names of cottages in the area. I couldn't think of one called Seaview. Unfortunately, when a cottage was sold, the new owner would often bestow it with a handle more to his liking.

"Is there a Seaview where you were digging?"

She shook her head glumly. "I didn't see one."

"How do you know the cottage was close to the water?"

"Gramps used to tell me he'd sit out on the porch while they were waiting for the smuggling ships and look out at the ocean. So, I figured it had to be one of those cottages near the water. And the name, too . . . Seaview."

"And why gold and not cash?"

"Gramps didn't say anything about why it was gold."

What she said about the cottage made sense, all right. But there was something tickling in the back of my mind. Between the hangover and the stress of almost getting whacked with a shovel, outrunning the cops and being exhausted, I couldn't unravel it right now. It would have to wait until morning.

"Can you help me, Dan?" she asked. "I'm rather lost." She hesitated. "I'd pay you. You can have twenty-five percent of the gold we find—if we find it. Would that be okay?"

I could use that money if it was really there. She and her boy needed the money, too. I'd be helping for an honorable reason. After all, I did know the beach like the back of my hand.

Besides, if I didn't help her, she might ask someone else—the wrong person—get ripped off or worse. More than a few bad characters on Hampton Beach. Without me, the chance of her finding the gold safely were slim. With me, the odds of a good outcome increased.

Helping out could end up costing me time and labor, though. Nice to think I'd be compensated. "Okay."

She beamed, stood up, and said, "Deal."

I got up and we shook on it. Then she said, "I might as well get going."

"Where's your car?" I asked.

"A few cottages down the street."

"It's late to drive to Boston."

"I rented a place on the beach . . . at the Sea Urchin." I knew the place, a run-down motel on Ashworth Ave.

"I'll walk you there then."

"No, just to my car is plenty," she said.

I reached for the door as something crossed my mind. "I might have to get a little help from a friend of mine. He knows more about what goes on around here than even I do.'

She looked at me with furrowed brows.

"Don't worry," I said, trying to reassure her. "I guarantee he won't say anything to anyone. I'll give him some of my share if we happen to find anything."

She looked doubtful and I thought she was going to nix the idea of my bringing a friend into the hunt, but she smiled slightly and shrugged.

We stepped outside. The night was old, the morning not quite dawning. I rarely saw this time of day. I liked it, though.

I walked Monica to her car—a beat-up old rattrap that looked like it wouldn't pass its next inspection. She grabbed a pen and paper from inside the car, scrawled her room number at the Urchin on it, and handed the paper to me. I watched as she drove down the street, took a right, and disappeared onto Ocean Boulevard.

Chapter 3

"GOLD, DANNY?" There was a bit of glaze in my best friend Shamrock Kelly's eyes.

It was around ten-thirty the morning after my run-in with Monica Nichols. Shamrock and I sat side by side at the bar of the High Tide Restaurant and Saloon. We were at the L-shaped end of the bar, opposite the big picture window that looked out on Ocean Boulevard and the Atlantic beyond. I'd just come in for my shift, interrupting my friend's morning perusal of the *Boston Herald* to tell him of my previous night's visitor.

"As you so often say, Shamrock, 'don't get your knickers in a twist' about it. We're talking only fifteen thousand dollars here."

"But that's plenty. And gold on Hampton Beach? Sweet Mother Mary." He looked dreamily toward the ceiling as he blew a smoke ring from his cigarette.

"There might not be any gold," I said. "This could be just the imagining of some old man suffering from dementia. Besides, I don't even know this woman. The whole thing could be B.S."

Shamrock grabbed my arm. "But if there is gold, Danny. Just think of it. You Yanks did outlaw God's nectar back in the day, did you not?"

"You know we did, but what's that prove?"

Shamrock grinned. "Well, there was a lot of booze smuggling. That could have involved payment in gold. Gold. On Hampton Beach."

"I suppose. But I've never heard of smuggling on this beach. At least not booze, and why would smugglers want to get paid in gold?"

Shamrock gave my arm a little shake. "I don't know, but there could have been smuggling, back in the day. It's possible."

"I suppose . . ."

"We're about as close as you can get to my homeland with our Irish whiskey . . ." Shamrock snorted, "and that other place with their scotch."

I knew Shamrock didn't mean Scotland. He meant England. His disdainful snort had told me that. Shamrock was no friend of England. Before he came to our beach years ago, he'd had a relationship with the Irish Republican Army. That's all I can say—I've been sworn to secrecy on the subject.

"I suppose so." I thought for a minute. "Still, it doesn't mean any of this is true. I've never heard anything about gold being buried here. It is pretty farfetched."

Shamrock tugged on my arm again. This time I gave him a look and brushed his hand away.

"But you said the lass seemed like a fine woman. And she has a needy boy. You did say that, Danny boy."

I shrugged and nodded. "I did."

"Then you've got to help her, Danny, for the boy's sake."
He waited a minute. When I didn't respond, he added, "And
what about the split she promised you?"

I shook my head. "Twenty-five percent of nothing is
nothing, Shamrock."

"Ahhh, get off your pity pot. This lassie and her boy
need help and I know you won't let her down. Besides, it
sounds like a fine adventure and with no danger involved to
boot. How can you say no to that?"

My friend knew me well. There was no way I could say
no. Monica had asked for my help, and she and her son
seemed to be down on their luck. I certainly believed her
story about hoping to get her son out of Charlestown. And
I could use a few thousand dollars, that was for sure. I'd
already decided that if I got involved in this treasure hunt,
I was going to need Shamrock's help. I'd split my share with
him, although I was still skeptical there would be anything
of value to divide.

"I can't," I finally said. "Say no, that is. Would you like to
help out? Or do I have to ask?"

Shamrock's ruddy face beamed. "Have I ever let you
down?"

I had to admit he never had let me down. Shamrock and
I had many adventures together on Hampton Beach and he'd
always had my back. Some of the situations we'd found ourselves involved in had been quite dicey, to say the least. But
here we both were, still in one piece.

I clapped his shoulder. "If we find anything of value, I'll
give you half of what I get."

"No, no, no, Danny. You don't have to do that."

"Okay," I said. "At least I offered."

Shamrock gave me a startled look. Then he saw a grin spread across my face.

He laughed. "You're quite the kidder, Danny boy. Always making with the funnies. Anything you think is fair will be fine."

After a long silence, he added, "Where do we start?"

"Not sure, but I have one small thing I want to check out." There was that little itch I'd had in the back of my brain when Monica had finished her tale. "I want to visit someone."

Shamrock thumped his chest with his beat-up thumb. "I'll come along for backup."

I chuckled. "Thanks, but no. I won't need backup on this stop."

"What should I do then?" Shamrock looked a little dejected. He didn't like being left out.

"Give me some time to come up with something. Don't worry. If you're getting a piece of the loot, I'm going to make sure you're doing your share of the work."

We both laughed.

Shamrock went back to smoking and reading his newspaper. I thought about what Monica had told me.

Before long, Shamrock cleared his throat. "Are you going to tell Dianne about this?"

Dianne? The person who'd bought the High Tide at auction back when I was about to lose the business because of my cocaine addiction? She'd kept me on as a bartender and helped me with my rehabilitation—what there was of it—along with Shamrock. She'd also let me maintain a very small ownership portion of the business. I'd always assumed it was because it would have looked curious if the business remained 'Dan Marlowe's High Tide Restaurant and Saloon.' Dianne wouldn't change that. She knew I'd put my heart and soul into building this business and it was all I had left. She would never kick me when I was down.

Dianne and I had a wonderful personal relationship at one time, too, until I screwed that up recently by falling off the cocaine wagon. She broke up with me and fired me from my job. Familiar with my rocky financial situation and my two kids—kids she was fond of—she'd bailed me out for a second time by hiring me back part time. Our personal situation had not improved though, although I hoped it might. I was trying as hard as I could and was determined to hold my demons at bay no matter what, hoping I could make it back to the time when the urges would diminish enough to control.

"No," I finally said. "And you aren't either. You know how she feels about me getting involved in stuff like this.

"Aye, Danny, I do." Shamrock nodded like a wise old man.

Someone pounded on the big wooden front door. I glanced up at the Clydesdale clock on the wall. Eleven o'clock. Time to open and I hadn't even set up the bar yet.

Shamrock folded his newspaper, stubbed his smoke out in the ashtray, and slid from his stool. "Your public's here, Danny."

I grabbed his arm as he walked by. "Let's not mention this to anyone, Shamrock, especially about what we're looking for. The last thing we want is a gold rush on Hampton Beach."

Shamrock ran his forefinger across his mouth. "My lips are sealed, Danny."

Chapter 4

"YOU'RE LATE AGAIN," were the first words I heard as I opened the front door of the High Tide and secured it with an eye hook.

Eli brushed past and headed for his usual stool, midway along the bar and opposite the beer spigots. He was up to my shoulders in height and a Camel cigarette bobbed up and down in his mouth as he spoke. He was a house painter by trade and was dressed accordingly—white pants, shirt, and cap, all paint-blotched.

Sauntering in right behind him was my other morning regular, Paulie. He was taller than me and thin with shoulder-length brown hair sprinkled with gray. He wore a light blue shirt with the patch of a postal worker over a pair of faded jeans.

He nodded as he passed. "Dan."

He went to the L-shaped end of the bar where Shamrock and I had just been sitting and slid onto a stool. I went around the bar, poured a Bud draft for Eli, and popped the cap off a Miller Lite for Paulie.

After I'd placed their drinks in front of them, I raced around the bar doing the chores I should have already done:

fill two sinks with ice, turn on two overhead televisions—one at each end of the bar—dice the fruit and placed it in the fruit tray along with onions and olives, spread ashtrays along the bar, and a few other preparations necessary for the daily opening of Hampton Beach's busiest and best bar. I refilled my two customers' drinks before they asked.

Eli and Paulie were halfway through their second beers by the time I finished my opening chores. As I knew they would, they started to come to life. The pair rarely spoke until deep into their second alcoholic beverage.

"Ahh," Eli said as he ran the sleeve of his paint-stained white shirt across his mouth to remove a small beer mustache. "That's better. I've already had a rough day."

Paulie chortled at the end of the bar. Behind him, through the picture window, I could see an occasional car passing on Ocean Boulevard. Now that Labor Day was history and the busy season had passed, traffic was light. We still did a good business, though, what with all the locals, our great reputation, and the fact that only a few restaurants on the beach remained open year round.

"What rough day?" Paulie asked. "Did you have to bring the rubbish to the curb in front of your house?" He puffed on a cigarette and blew perfect smoke rings toward the ceiling where they erupted on contact.

Eli raised his scrawny body. "Very funny. I'll have you know, I was awfully busy this morning."

Paulie snickered. "It certainly didn't have anything to do with painting. You haven't held a paint brush in your hand for years."

Eli's eyes widened and his face flushed redder than a beet. "You know I'm semi-retired."

"Drop the semi part and I know it," Paul said with a grin.

Eli chugged the remainder of his beer, then waved the nine-ounce Pilsner glass in my direction and jiggled it. I filled a fresh glass from the spigot— leaving a very small foamy head—and placed the glass on a cocktail napkin in front of him.

Eli looked at the beer and ran his tongue over his thin lips. "I'll have you know, I'm very choosy on the work I accept." He kept his eyes on the beer.

"Hah!" Paulie didn't waste time with his comeback. "You wouldn't accept the job of painting a doghouse. A small doghouse."

Eli furrowed his brows, glaring in Paulie's direction. "Weisenheimer. Why don't you get a goddamn haircut?"

Paulie said, as usual, "Because it's my trademark."

"Trademark, shmademark," Eli said. "You look like the last of the hippies. Like a damn fool."

This little back and forth occurred every morning when my first two customers of the day showed up. It was part of their daily ritual, along with the exact number of beers each consumed, and the time they left every day.

The dialogue altered, of course, but not much. If you were here enough days in a row, as I was, you'd hear the same stories repeated every few days. It grew old fast. About this time each day I got tired of their back and forth, and I'd attempt to change the conversation. Today, though, I had last night's encounter with Monica Nichols on my mind and couldn't think of much else to say.

I'd be playing with fire if I brought it up now. Eli and Paulie were very perceptive men, and Eli had a gossip-mongering problem to boot. He was as nosy as a person could be and would spread rumors faster than cars heading for the lone empty parking spot on a summer weekend day.

Still, they both knew Hampton Beach well. If I kept the talk discreet—and didn't mention the word 'gold'—I should be safe. The last thing I wanted was for Eli to know there was a possibility that glittering metal was hidden somewhere in our little oceanside village. He'd blab the information around the beach faster than you could get a sunburn on the first sunny July day. I had to watch myself, but this was as good a place as any to start my inquiries.

I cleared my throat. "Hey, you guys ever hear of any smuggling going on around here?"

"Smuggling? Smuggling?" Eli asked. You'd think I'd asked him to explain one of Einstein's theories.

"I heard that Blackbeard buried treasure on the Isle of Shoals way back when," Paulie said. "That what you mean?"

I shook my head. "No, no. I meant liquor. Booze. Back during Prohibition."

Eli squinted at me suspiciously. "Why you wanna know that?"

I had to think fast. "I was reading an old book about Prohibition and rumrunners. Wondered if anything like that happened around here?"

Eli's eyes softened a bit. "I ain't ever heard about any-thing like that. Of course, I ain't old enough to know about that stuff."

"What?" Paulie said. "You're *older* than dirt, *old* man."

Eli batted his hand in Paulie's direction. "Put a sock in it, will ya?"

Paulie laughed loudly.

Eli took a sip of his beer, set the glass down, and snapped his fingers. "Hey, wait a minute. Smuggling? What about that boat that ran up on the jetty? Remember that?"

Yes, I did, and I didn't like the direction this conversation was going. I may have really put my foot in my mouth by bringing it up. Trouble was coming—from a different direction than I'd considered. If there was one thing I didn't want resurrected, it was anything that would link my name with the substance that had caused most of the trouble in my life—cocaine.

Before I could jump in, Eli said, "It was loaded with cocaine, wasn't it? Yeah, cocaine. And two murdered guys." He pointed a thin, bony finger at me. "Remember? You was mixed up in that, Dan."

Yes, I had been, but not on the wrong side of the law as Eli made it sound. Still, if the conversation continued on this track, the story would make the rounds again, linking my name with the drug I was trying hard to stay far away from, and maybe damage my semi-rehabbed reputation again.

Down at the other end of the bar, Paulie seemed to be studying the decor, looking at everything except me.

I was trying to come up with something that would derail this line of chatter. I was rescued by a group of boisterous town workers coming through the front door on their lunch break. The half-dozen men took stools at the bar between Eli and Paulie. I hurried to place setups and menus in front of them, then I busied myself with their drink orders.

I'd luckily escaped the rehashing of old news by Eli— old news I'd prefer was forgotten. I didn't have to worry about that now. I'd be busy with a steady stream of lunch customers and have no free time to converse with either Eli or Paulie. They'd each have a few more beers and leave on schedule.

I'd almost stepped in it by approaching Eli and Paulie for info and learned nothing about the puzzle concerning Monica's grandfather.

I still had the little tickle in the back of my head, though, the tickle that started when Monica told me her tale. As I'd mentioned to Shamrock, I knew who might be able to scratch that itch.

Chapter 5

"HELLO, CORA. CAN I speak to you a minute?"

I'd left the High Tide at the end of my shift and stopped at a small brown one-story cottage on my way home. The cottage sat on the same side of the street as mine, a few buildings farther from the beach.

"Of course you can, Daniel." Cora Petit sat in a wicker rocking chair and patted the seat of a twin rocker beside her. She'd called me 'Daniel' since I was a little boy. "Come right up here."

I walked up three stairs to the porch and plunked myself down beside her.

"You always greet me when you walk by, Daniel, but it's been a long time since you've stopped for a chat."

Cora was a tiny woman with pure white hair worn in a bun on her head. Her blue eyes were clear and filled with sparkle, and her skin had few wrinkles for a woman her age. I chalked that up to a clean lifestyle and genes along with the positive attitude she always seemed to generate. I knew her age was somewhere around eighty, but she was still sharp as a tack.

"Working up the Tide a lot, Cora. Have to keep busy and pay bills."

"Well, that's one thing I don't have to worry about, Daniel. I don't have to worry if I have enough money for bills. Henri made sure of that, bless his soul." Henri was her long-deceased husband.

"How've you been, Cora?"

"Fine. Fine. I enjoy the fall. Not as hectic as summer and the weather is so nice." She rubbed her hands gently together on her lap. Despite what she'd said about the weather, she wore a long, black wool skirt and a blue button-up sweater over a white blouse.

Cora's father had built many of the early cottages in this area known as the "Island"—way back before I was ever here—and she had summered here since she was small. If anyone remembered the early history of this area, it would be Cora Petit. We exchanged small talk for a while before I got down to business.

I knew that my cottage and a couple of the cottages adjacent to it had been constructed around 1950. Before that there had been nothing but sand where they now stood—as far as I knew. I didn't know about the cottages in front of mine, though. There were two or three between my place and the beach itself. I asked Cora if she knew when they had been built.

"Hmmm," Cora said, gazing off in the direction of the beach for a minute. "1940s maybe? Why?"

"I was just trying to find out what cottages were around here, say in 1930."

She tried to snap her fingers. "Ouch."

She straightened her gnarled fingers.

"That's easy. This camp," she pointed with her thumb over her shoulder, "and the one back there were built in 1920 by my father, Emile."

I knew the term 'camp' had been used decades ago instead of cottage and gave her an encouraging smile without saying anything.

"Those were the first cottages on this side of the street." She leaned forward in her rocker, looked down the street in the direction of the beach, and made a wide sweeping motion with her arm.

"There was nothing between here and the ocean back then. This was an oceanfront camp at that time, although there was an empty lot here in front of us for a short bit. I remember my mother always criticizing my father for not buying it cheap when he had the chance, but he was a conservative man. Didn't like being in debt. Something was built there, though I can't remember when, but the building didn't last long. It was destroyed in a winter nor'easter, I think. And the building that's there now . . . was built later."

"What year was this, Cora? What was the first building called?"

Cora rubbed her hands together as if she were washing them. They sounded like sandpaper, they were so dry. "Oh, Daniel. I'm so sorry. I just can't remember. Give me a few days to think and maybe talk to the girls."

'The girls' were a group of elderly women who lived in the area and got together at each other's houses on a weekly basis. I was chomping at the bit now and would have pushed harder if Cora had been forty years younger. But she wasn't. She was a wonderful person, so I held myself in check and decided to let her go at her own pace.

This was the first bit of good information I'd received regarding my search. If the cottages closer to the beach hadn't even been around in 1930, it could only mean that Monica's grandfather had been staying in a building further back from the water than she'd thought. She had definitely been off in her digging.

A small sign hung a few inches from the top of Cora's front porch identifying her cottage's name, Summer Breeze. I knew the cottage behind hers was the Irish . . . something or other. Either could have had different names in the past.

"Was there ever a cottage around here called Seaview?"

She pursed her lips for a moment. "That's probably a common name on the beach. Sounds good for potential renting, but around here?" She rubbed a very faint white stubble on her chin, pondering the question for a couple of minutes. "I don't think so, Daniel. There could have been one back when I was a young girl. Children don't really notice that kind of thing, you know, unless it's their camp. I certainly know none of the cottages my father built on this street were called Seaview. I can't say about the others. Why do you want to know?"

I hated lying to Cora. Even though she was known to be tight-lipped—the exact opposite of my beer customer Eli—I still didn't dare mention *that* word. "Just doing some research about the street, Cora. You know, the old days here. I've always wondered about them."

She gave me a sly look but seemed to accept my explanation. "Oh, Daniel, they were wonderful days back then. Everyone was friendly and we all knew each other."

She gazed off toward the ocean. Her eyes began to mist. "It was the most wonderful time of my life." She turned toward me. "Did you know I met Henri here? Right on this beach?"

"No, I didn't."

She told me a beautiful tale—the story of meeting her husband during a summer long ago, only steps down from here, on the sand. As she spoke, I realized this story could be told by thousands of people who'd had similar experiences on this little strip of land—Hampton Beach. I didn't interrupt her. I listened to it all and thoroughly enjoyed it.

When she was done, she dabbed at her eyes with a tissue she pulled from her sweater cuff.

"So much fun, Daniel. But so, so long ago." She gave her head a little shake. "You're a young man. I shouldn't have bored you with my sad story. I rarely talk about it with young people. I'm sorry."

I certainly wasn't young, although compared to Cora I guess I was. "I loved every word of it, Cora. I like hearing about the old days on the beach." This was a good time to move along. "Do you mind if I ask you more questions about the beach back in the day if I think of any?"

She reached over and gently touched my arm. "Of course not, Daniel. You stop by anytime. I love to have the company."

"Thanks, Cora. I'd better get going."

She took her hand from my arm as I stood.

"I'll see you later." The porch stairs thumped like a hollow drum as I walked down the steps to the street.

She waved as I walked away. "Goodbye, Daniel."

On the short walk to my cottage, I mulled over what I'd learned from Cora Petit—none of the cottages I was walking past had existed in 1930. That meant Monica's grandfather hadn't been referring to any of them as the cottage he'd been staying in, a cottage with buried gold one hundred feet from it. What cottage, Seaview or whatever it might have been called, could he have been alluding to? I had no idea. Still, Cora had cleared up part of the mystery and given me an idea where my next lead might come from.

Chapter 6

I WAS STILL mulling over what I'd learned when I stepped into my cottage—and found a mess.

My place had been tossed, but not professionally.

It didn't take me more than a minute of surveying my cottage to determine that. It was thorough, though; my home was a disaster.

Too bad I didn't have my revolver on me, it might have helped with my rising anxiety. But the revolver was in the front bedroom, my bedroom, in the nightstand drawer. It might as well have been on the roof of the cottage next door for all the good it was doing.

Cushions had been knocked askew on both the sofa and my easy chair. The doors of the television cabinet gaped open and the contents scattered across the floor. Rows of knickknacks, mostly nautical, displayed in an old bookcase had been disturbed, some tipped over.

My bedroom wasn't any neater. The mattress was partially on the floor, indicating someone had taken a peek beneath it. Bureau drawers were open, clothing littered on the floor. I was happy to find the .38 revolver where I'd left it. 'Betsy,' my double-barreled shotgun, was still under my bed.

My anxiety eased slightly when I found my Xanax, used to control my anxiety condition, still stuffed in a sock. I had a feeling I'd be needing a pill's help before too long. My anxiety was just beginning to reach an uncomfortable level—my heartbeat quickened and my palms began to sweat. A feeling of impending doom settled over me. I was convinced this anxiety disorder was a result of my past cocaine addiction, but it didn't really matter, not at this point.

I took one of the pills from the bottle and let it dissolve beneath my tongue. Within five minutes the unpleasant symptoms began to recede.

The kitchen and bathroom had also been searched. The other two small bedrooms, my children's when they visited, hadn't been overlooked either. Nothing seemed to be missing though.

That got me thinking. The only things I had of value were my guns and the television and that was about it. I hadn't had many toys since my life had gone sour years ago. Cottages around this area had been the targets of break-ins for years, especially during the off-season when many were empty. Generally, the perpetrators were junkies or kids. My guns and TV were still here—that told me it hadn't been a junkie. A junkie would have scooped up those items in a New York minute.

That left kids.

I went back into the kitchen and looked in the fridge. Two bottom bins had been removed, the vegetables and overripe fruit scattered across the floor. Like I said, whoever it was had been very thorough—even checking inside my kitchen appliances. Everything was still there, including my beer. Yes, it was all there—two cold six-packs of Heineken. I was a kid once and had no doubt if my ransacker had been a young person, the beer would have been history.

If not junkies or kids, then who? And why?

I called Shamrock, then made a double run through the cottage, confirming my first conclusion that nothing was missing.

Chapter 7

THAT'S WHEN THE front door opened and Shamrock stepped in, wearing his restaurant whites.

He slapped his forehead. "For the love a Mary, Danny. You weren't kidding when you said your place had been trashed. What happened here?"

I looked around at the mess. "I had a visitor."

"You had more than a visitor. You had a wrecking crew, goddammit. This happened while you were at work?"

"Must have," I answered. "It was okay when I left this morning." I picked a few items off the floor and shoved them back into the bottom of the television cabinet.

"Did they steal anything?" Shamrock rearranged the cushions on the sofa, then picked up a few of my cheap nautical knickknacks and returned them to the bookcase.

"Nothing that I can see."

"Your hardware?" Shamrock asked, referring to my guns.

"Both there." I busied myself picking up more knickknacks.

"How did the blackguards get in?"

I hadn't even thought of that. I walked to the door, examined the lock. It hadn't been disturbed. Neither had the window that faced the porch. I walked through the kitchen and took a peek at the back door. It hadn't been tampered with, either. That left one more possible entry point.

My bedroom had a window that opened onto the front porch. Bingo! The screen on the window had been removed.

I'd left the window itself unlocked, as I often did. I stuck my head outside and spotted my damaged screen over on the far left side of the porch. I hadn't noticed it when I'd first come home.

"They ripped off the screen, slid the window open," I said, coming back into the front room. "Got in that way."

"Well, if a screen is all you lost, Danny, you got out of it cheap."

I headed to the kitchen, grabbed two beers from the fridge, opened them, and carried one to Shamrock.

"You want help with the kitchen and bedrooms?"

"No, no. I'll get to them later." I waved Shamrock to the couch while I took my easy chair.

"Who would have done this, Danny? Break in and take nothing. And in broad daylight for the love a God."

I took a long pull on the beer. "I don't know. It's strange. Like you said—daytime and nothing missing. Someone was searching for something."

One possibility came to mind.

Shamrock mentioned it first. "What about the lassie . . . Monica . . . what was her name?"

"Monica Nichols," I said slowly.

"Aye, Danny. She was here just last night. Then this happens. Quite a coincidence if you ask me."

Shamrock was right, of course. It was quite a coincidence. Beyond that, there were a couple of other things connected to Monica Nichols' late night visit to my area of Hampton Beach still troubling me.

Why had she been so quick to cut me in on her gold hunt? Had it really been that she was completely lost as to where she should search?

And how did she know I wouldn't look for the gold on my own time, keep it for myself?

There was only one way to find the answers.

"You want to take a walk down Ashworth Avenue with me?"

"To where this Monica is staying?"

I nodded. "That's right."

"She won't get spooked? Me knowing about the gold, Danny?"

I shook my head. "I already told her you were going to be included."

Shamrock nodded. "Let's go then."

We finished our beers and headed to Monica Nichols' temporary digs. What we'd find out, I had no idea.

Chapter 8

THE SEA URCHIN was located on the ocean side of Ashworth Avenue. Old and a bit rundown, it was similar to many of the motels in this area of Hampton Beach. The blue-and-white two-story wood structure was one of many motels on the beach that offered off-season rentals by the week or month. A rougher crowd than the summer tourists who occupied the rooms in the expensive summer months took advantage of the cheap winter rates.

Shamrock and I took the stairs to the second floor and continued along a walkway, searching for number 214, the room Monica had written on the paper she'd handed me. We found it midway.

I gave Shamrock a sidelong glance, then rapped on the door.

Within moments, Monica answered. She looked as she had before, but this time dressed in a red blouse and white baggy shorts. Her feet were bare.

"Dan," she said, although it was Shamrock she was staring at. She glanced quickly at his restaurant whites. I think his garb threw her.

Quickly, I said, "This is the friend I told you about, Monica. My best friend, Michael Kelly."

She hesitated, then opened the door all the way and stepped aside. "Come on in."

"You can call me Shamrock," my friend said as we walked in.

The inside of the small studio with kitchenette unit didn't have anything to distinguish it from dozens of similar places I'd seen on the beach throughout the years.

We stood in the single main room, which had two cheap, black vinyl armchairs side by side; both were well-worn. A large brown couch sat directly across from the chairs. It looked as worn as the chairs and likely pulled out into an uncomfortable double bed. A small table with a lamp was situated between the two chairs. A second table and lamp sat at the far end of the sofa.

Off to the left was a very tight kitchen area with a tiny sink and a two-burner stove not much wider than a yard stick. Squeezed in was one of those miniature fridges you see in college dorms.

The unit was not messy. Monica apparently did the best she could with what she had.

"Anything to drink?" Monica asked.

Shamrock glanced at me.

"No, we're fine," I said.

Monica headed for the couch while Shamrock and I took the adjoining chairs.

"Have you found where . . ." she hesitated, glancing at Shamrock.

I assured her again that her secret—our secret now—was safe with my friend.

She sighed and seemed to accept that, not that she had much choice. "Do you know where . . . we need to look?"

"I'm not that good or that fast."

"Then what's up?" She asked, looking at me warily. "Just come by to say hi?"

I got the sense that she already had an idea. Then again maybe it was my imagination. "I had a visitor earlier today while I was at work. Or maybe visitors."

"Oh," she said.

Her eyes seemed to hold a glimmer of dread. Was it really there or was it my imagination again? "Somebody broke into my cottage and tore the place apart."

I tried to gauge her reaction. She was mum. A little too mum. Her eyes didn't blink and she barely seemed to breathe. I cleared my throat.

"Where were you today, Monica?"

"Me?" She pointed at her chest, indignant. "You think I broke into your house?"

I shook my head. "Someone did."

"I wouldn't break into your goddamn house." She leaned forward in her seat. "Who the hell do you think I am?"

I glanced at Shamrock, though I don't know why. Maybe for a little support. He wasn't going to be any help, though. He'd become involved in an extensive study of the motel unit's chintzy decor.

I tried to keep my voice calm. "Look, I just met you, just heard your story about . . ."

Monica looked like a stone statue.

"About the gold buried here on Hampton Beach."

"There is gold buried here," Monica finally said. "I wouldn't lie to you."

"I know," I said, even though I was anything but sure of that fact. "Still, it's a pretty big coincidence that my house was broken into and searched right after you told me all this."

"Things like the happen all the time where I live."

I tried another tack. "Does anyone else know about the gold besides you, Monica?"

"No. No one." She said it too fast. "Nobody else knows. How could anyone know? I didn't tell anyone. Did you tell anyone?"

Nice try. She wasn't going to turn the tables that easily though. I was almost certain that someone else knew of the gold and Monica Nichols knew who that someone was. I decided to call her bluff.

"All right, then," I said. "I can't work in the dark. You can forget our deal." I stood. "Come on, Shamrock. We're going."

Shamrock had a puzzled look on his face but he stood. I turned for the door.

"So you're going to look for the gold yourself," she said. "You bastard. I knew I shouldn't have trusted you."

I turned back. "You may not believe me, but I'm not going to look for your gold. If you find it, it's all yours."

She started wringing her hands in her lap. "Okay. I know who it *might* have been." She glanced away then stared down at her hands. "But it probably wasn't him. He doesn't know I'm here . . . I don't think. Please. Sit down."

We did. I waited for a minute while she played with her hands some more. Before she could wear them out, I said, "All right, Monica. Who else knows about it?"

You would think I was going to yank out one of her front teeth, the way she looked at me. She didn't want to give up the information. Eventually, she shrugged. "It might be my brother, Billy."

That wasn't as bad as I'd started imagining. Her hesitancy to spill the name at first had me conjuring up visions of monsters and zombies hot on the trail of the gold. A brother named Billy I could deal with.

"How does he know about it?"

She shook her head. "I'm not sure he does know. I didn't tell him. If he knows about the gold, he doesn't know it's here. He only—"

I interrupted. "If he's the one who broke into my place, he knows."

She licked her lips, looking more than a bit frantic. "How could he?"

"Followed you here, lass," Shamrock said, speaking for the first time since we'd arrived. "He must have seen you at Dan's cottage somehow."

"But . . . he couldn't have," Monica said. "I tried to make sure no one followed me when I left my car."

I gave that a moment's thought. "He had to see you leave then. He probably followed you to where you were digging. When the cops started showing up, he stayed out of sight. Came back later and kept an eye on your car. He would've seen me walking you to it. Would've been easy for him to follow me back, especially if he moved along behind the cottages on the opposite side of the street."

"That's it, Danny," Shamrock said excitedly. "That's how this eejit . . . excuse me, miss—your brother . . . found out where Danny lives."

I narrowed my eyes as I stared at Monica. "But how did he find out about the gold in the first place? And who else knows?"

Monica shook her head again. "No one. No one else knows. I swear."

I took that oath with a grain of salt. "And exactly how did he find out?"

Monica let out a long sigh. "I told you. My grandfather came to live with me near the end. Well . . . B . . . Billy was . . . in between apartments and he came to live with me for a couple of weeks. He must have heard Gramps talking to me about the gold or Gramps told him something when I was out. Billy asked me about it a few times. I played dumb. Said Gramps was a senile old man and it was just his imagination. I don't know if he believed me or not. But . . . Billy's . . . I guess you'd say, street smart. He wouldn't let it go. And hasn't since Gramps died."

"Okay," I said. "So, your brother knows about the gold and he puts enough stock in your grandfather's words to follow you here and wreck my cottage looking for . . . what?"

"Maybe he thinks you and Monica are connected somehow," Shamrock said. "He might not know that you just bumped into each other. That way he might think you had information about the location of gold in your cottage. A map, maybe?"

"Makes sense." I turned back to Monica. "But he is your brother. You don't want to share the gold with him?"

Monica's eyes grew to the size of poker chips. "My brother?" She caught herself and shifted gears. "No, not with him." She chewed her lip before continuing. "He has a little drug problem and he'd just spend it on that shit. Besides, I told you why I need that gold. For Sam."

I could read between the lines enough to realize her brother, Billy, was probably a drug addict who'd go through his share of money as fast as he could buy the dope. Probably try to get Monica's gold and her son's share, too. Keeping him out of the loop made sense. I'd do the same.

"Okay," I said. "At least now I've got an idea who broke into my place and what we're up against."

Shamrock straightened in his chair. "He doesn't sound like much." To Monica he said, "Excuse me, lass, but I'll give this brother o' yours a good thumping if he even looks at Danny's house again."

Monica shuddered at Shamrock's statement, though I wasn't sure why. We'd solved the mystery of my homewrecker. That was all there was to it—I hoped.

Chapter 9

LATE THE NEXT morning, I picked Shamrock up at his cottage. He'd finished his early shift and we both had the rest of the day off. Even though Dianne had rehired me, I had lost a couple of shifts in my short absence. Although I hoped to make them up eventually, I wasn't betting everything on it. I considered myself fortunate that Dianne was even talking to me after our last falling out. All my fault, of course.

"Where are we off to?" Shamrock asked. He was riding shotgun in my little green Chevette as we tooled along Ocean Boulevard. Off-season meant the traffic was light, even though it was a picture-perfect day with temperatures around seventy degrees. Except for a few white, puffy clouds, the sky was a mass of beautiful blue, blending in with the ocean to our right. There were a fair number of pedestrians and a couple dozen shops and other businesses open, taking advantage of the weather.

"The library."

"The library?" Shamrock sounded as if I'd said we were headed for the Roman Colosseum. "What are we going there for?"

"Research," I said. "I figure if there was a shootout with a death on Hampton Beach, it had to be covered in the newspapers. Maybe we'll get a hint of where to look for the . . . you know."

A cacophony of bells and whistles sounded from the Casino as we passed. A very nice gray-haired wisp of a woman, who always wore a kerchief on her head, ran the iconic shooting gallery situated in the center of the building. Some said the kerchief was to conceal the earplugs she wore while working to protect her hearing from the incessant racket. I had no idea if that was true or not.

"Ahh, Danny, I thought we were going somewhere exciting. I'm not good at research. You know I don't like it." Shamrock gave me a side glance. "You sure you need me?"

"Yes, I do. If you think you're going to get a piece of this treasure by only coming along on the fun parts of the hunt, you're mistaken. Research can be time consuming, and with your help, maybe I can chop the time in half."

"All right," Shamrock said, sighing. "I guess you got to take the bad with the good."

A few minutes later, I took a left onto Winnacunnet Road. A couple of minutes after that, I took a right and parked near the side entrance of the Lane Memorial Library, a one-story brick building that fronted on Winnacunnet Road in the Town of Hampton proper. Shamrock and I got out of the car and walked inside. There was a long, wooden reception desk, similar to reception desks in every other library I'd been in. On the far side of the desk sat the librarian. She wore a badge on a lanyard identifying her as Alice Athens.

She had striking silver hair and was somewhere between fifty and sixty, very attractive for her age. She looked at me over glasses perched on the end of her nose.

"May I help you?"

"Yes," I answered. "I'm Dan Marlowe. I called yesterday about some old newspapers. 1930."

"Oh, Mr. Marlowe, you were very lucky. We had some books come in this morning from Boston Public and they included your requested issues. They are on micro fiche, of course."

Made sense to me. "Thank you."

"I'll be back shortly," she said as she scurried off to get my requested items.

Shamrock followed me to a small seating area with magazine racks. I grabbed a copy of *Time* and he took an issue of—what else—*Irish Life*. We took seats and flipped pages while we waited for the attractive librarian.

Mercifully, it didn't take as long as I feared it might. Within five minutes, Alice returned to the reception desk with a small box in her hand. She motioned for us to follow, then turned and walked away. She had on a tight black skirt that showed off a nice rear. Nicest I'd ever seen on a librarian anyway.

Shamrock and I hurried to catch up. In a far corner of the library, she pulled out two chairs that belonged to twin machines, both situated on a long metal desk. I knew what the machines were—Shamrock and I had done research on them once before—but didn't remember how to use them.

Alice set the box on the desk between the machines. Stenciled on top of the box were the words, *Boston Globe Jan-Dec 1930*. She opened the box. "Is there a certain month you'd like to start with?"

I had given that some thought already. Between what Monica Nichols had told me and my knowledge of Hampton

Beach during the on and off seasons, I had quickly eliminated the summer months—too many prying eyes for smuggling booze and burying gold. I discarded the winter months when the Atlantic would have been too treacherous for smuggling operations, not to mention the snow-covered sand and the scarcity of winterized cottages in those early years.

"April to start," I said.

Alice sorted through the canisters in the box until she found the date she was looking for. She quickly pulled out the canister and removed its cover, sliding free a film cylinder. She unwound the film a few inches and proceeded to demonstrate the loading procedure on one of the machines. She attached the roll of film to one spool holder, fed the film into another, gave the crank a couple of turns, flicked a light switch, and—presto—the front page of a newspaper showed up on the machine's screen. Sure enough, it was the April 1, 1930, issue of the *Boston Globe*.

Alice repeated the process with another roll of film on the opposite machine. May 1, 1930. When she had my assurance that we understood how to operate the contraptions, she left us alone. I sat with the month of April; Shamrock took May.

"Do we have to go through every page, Danny?" Shamrock asked.

"I don't know. I guess it'd be on the front page, with a cop killed and all. But who knows? This front page seems to have nothing but news on the economy."

"Aye, Danny, same here. And the news ain't good. Nothing about any gunplay either. Too depressing about the economy. I'm going to turn the page . . . ahh, that's better. Here's a story about a raid on an opium den in Chinatown.

Let's see. 'Boston Police, along with Federal Narcotics Agents, stormed Ling Le Restaurant on Harrison Avenue near Ping On Alley. Authorities said—'"

"Interesting, Shamrock," I interrupted. "But let's find what we came for. I don't want to be here all day."

An hour later, after going through the spring months and being entertained by Shamrock's colorful but whispered swearing and bumbling with loading and unloading of spools, I finally hit pay dirt.

Right on the front page. Not the headline but what looked like it would be just below the fold. The September 28th issue. "I got it!"

Shamrock jumped up and peered over my shoulder.

COP KILLED IN BLOODY NH SHOOTOUT

One brave New Hampshire state policeman, Cpl. O'Malley, was killed as Federal Agents and State Police raided a beach cottage in Hampton Beach, New Hampshire, which held a ruthless gang of liquor smugglers intent on landing their contraband on a beach many of our readers are familiar with. The desperados were foiled when the stouthearted lawmen learned of their nefarious plans. With the summer cottage surrounded, the bootleggers were offered a chance to surrender. Refusing the offer, most of the criminal element were killed in jig time by heroic law enforcement officers and their Tommy guns. Only one of the evildoers survived, and he was taken away in

handcuffs. Unfortunately, the brave New Hampshire state policeman lost his life in the fearless
charge of the dwelling. Authorities say—

"This goes on for pages," I said to Shamrock, who was
still peering over my shoulder. "Let's see if there is any way
we can copy this."

We sought out Alice and discovered the article we wanted could be printed. She helped us with the task. Before we
left, I checked out a couple of books on prohibition and rum
running.

On the ride back to the beach, Shamrock looked at me.
"Do you think anything in the article will help us, Danny?"

"I'm not sure. But at least it clears up one thing I was
worried about."

"If Monica was tellin' a tale," Shamrock said, "about the
gunfight so long ago?"

I nodded. "That's right. At least now we know that part
of her story was on the up-and-up. When we get home, I'll
read the article through and see if it says anything about the
gold."

Chapter 10

THE NEXT MORNING I was just about ready to head to my shift at the High Tide when I heard the engine of what sounded like a hillbilly's car coming down my street. Eventually the noise stopped. Car doors slammed and a minute later footsteps thudded up my porch stairs, followed by a knock on the door. I opened the inner wooden door and wished I hadn't.

Eddie Hoar stood on my porch. Behind him stood his partner-in-crime, Derwood Doller.

Eddie and Derwood were a pair of long-time, small-time beach hustlers. Shamrock and I had inadvertently gotten mixed up with them a few times in the past during various beach shenanigans. Things had always turned out okay in the end. Never because of Eddie and Derwood—in spite of them.

I sighed. "Hey, Eddie. Derwood." I didn't open the screen door.

"Dan, my man," Eddie said, a fake smile on his thin, pockmarked face. His black-and-gray hair was plastered against his head with either gel or grease, I couldn't tell

which. His wardrobe was . . . out of the disco-era is descrip-
tion enough. He wore a thick gold chain around his scrawny
neck. The line of green on his skin under the chain indicated
the gold was fake. But what really caught my attention was
the shiner on Eddie's eye—it was a whopper. His right eye
was effectively closed by a bulging lid the size and color of a
small eggplant.

Derwood mumbled a greeting. He was a much larger figure in both girth and height. I could tell by his bowl-like hair
that he still went in for amateur barbers. Baggy jeans and a
gray sweatshirt hacked off at the elbows was about it for his
wardrobe. He was the dumb muscle of the duo and usually
followed whatever Eddie said. Eddie was the brains, barely,
of the two.

I just stared at them through the screen. When it became
obvious I wasn't going to invite them in, Eddie said, "Mind
if we come in for a minute, Dan?"

I felt like answering truthfully, but I was curious as to
what had a late sleeper like Eddie Hoar up and out of bed
in the morning and paying me a visit to boot. I hoped it had
nothing to do with his eye, but I feared that was too much
to ask. I slowly opened the screen door and stepped aside as
they entered.

Eddie immediately plunked down in my easy chair.
Anyone else I would have overlooked it but Eddie Hoar?

"My chair, Eddie," I said. "Up."

"Sure, sure, Dan. No problem." Eddie bounded up from
the chair and joined Derwood on the couch.

I took my chair, pleased that I hadn't given him any time
to fart in it. Derwood shifted around, studying the walls.
He was a big man, and I'd seen him in action before. He

could handle himself. His nervousness—along with the condition of Eddie's eye—made my anxiety level creep up. I was determined to hold my curiosity, though, and let Eddie tell me why he was here. When Eddie Hoar showed up at your house unannounced, it wasn't to deliver a Publisher's Clearing House check. I just hoped the reason behind the visit wouldn't be too bad.

"How was your summer, my man?" Eddie asked.

"Fine."

"I heard you were working at the Tide again."

I nodded. "Yup."

"How's Shamrock?"

"Good."

"You back with Dianne?"

"Look, Eddie, I have to get to work." I pointed at the plastic 'antique' ship's clock on the wall. "Can the small talk. What's up?"

Eddie held up his hands. "Whoa, whoa, Dan. All right." He glanced at Derwood . . . who quickly went back to studying the walls. "Me and Derwood got a little problem."

That caused Derwood to lose his interest in the walls. "I ain't got no problem, Eddie . . . well, I didn't until you got me mixed up in it. Now you got me in deep trouble."

"Shut up, Dumwood," Eddie said.

Derwood balled his big fist. "Don't call me that, Eddie. I'm already mad enough to knock your block off."

"Easy, Derwood, not here in my house," I said.

Eddie cowered away from Derwood. "Can't you take a joke? I'm just kiddin'."

Derwood lowered his fist. "I don't like your jokes, Eddie. Especially after the trouble you got me into."

"Did you do that?" I asked Derwood, nodding toward Eddie and his damaged eye. Whoever'd hit Eddie hadn't held back. But with all the grief I'd seen Eddie give Derwood through the years, I'd never known the big man to give Eddie more than what you could call a love tap. The guy who poked Eddie this time hadn't been worried about causing long-term damage. That was obvious.

"Not me . . . Dan . . . a crazy man . . . and he's gonna kill us both . . . if we . . . don't . . . help him." Derwood ran his words together and was short of breath at the same time.

Which didn't help my own anxiety. I took a trip to my bedroom, opened my sock drawer, and popped a Xanax under my tongue, hoping to ward off the panic attack I could feel coming on.

A minute later, back in my easy chair and feeling better, I gave Eddie an irritated look. "Who's going to kill you?"

His color paled and his hands shook.

I raised my voice. "Who's going to kill you, Eddie?"

I thought I already knew the answer but I had to ask. Maybe with luck, I'd be wrong.

Derwood finally answered. "Butchy Dunn. It's fuckin' Butchy Dunn." He couldn't have had more fear in his voice if the name had been Whitey Bulger.

I felt a sudden sense of dread and my heart raced. The anxiety I felt now was too much for the one pill I'd taken. I cleared my throat and tried to conceal my apprehension. I don't know if it worked or not. It might be a stretch, but . . .

"This Butchy Dunn. Does he go by the name Billy?" I asked.

"I did hear someone call him that once," Eddie answered, his voice shaking. "You know him, Dan?"

Monica Nichols' brother. I just knew it.

"No, different guy," I said, even though that wasn't true. But I wasn't going to give these two any more info than I had to, not until I knew what was going on, especially now that things had taken a more dangerous turn. Eddie's swollen eye and the terror on the faces of these two men told me the stakes were much higher than I'd thought.

"He's a killer, Dan," Derwood said. "And he's after you. He wants us to help him or he'll do that," He pointed at Eddie's bad eye, "and a lot worse to both of us if we don't."

"After me?" I raised an eyebrow. "For what? What the hell are you two talking about?"

"Come on, Dan," Eddie pleaded. "You gotta help us. If you don't, Butchy'll kill us. If we're lucky." I could actually see Eddie's body shaking. "It was me who wanted to come over here and give you a head's up."

"You lying sack of shit. " Derwood reached over and smacked Eddie on the head.

Eddie threw up his hands and howled.

"I told you I was comin' to warn Dan, even if you didn't want to go," Derwood said. "You don't care about Dan. And you had the bright idea to break into . . ."

"That was you?" I asked, looking squarely at Eddie.

Eddie held up his hands, palms out. "I didn't have any choice, Dan. He told us to find out what we could about what you and his sister were looking for. You don't know Butchy . . . he's bad." His eyes, even the swollen one, opened wide.

I didn't really want to hear it, but I had to know what I was up against. "Tell me about him."

"I met him when I was away at college," Eddie said.

"He means jail," Derwood said.

"I know that," I said. "Eddie, come on, tell me about him."

"Well, I was doing thirty days up in Rockingham County Jail." Eddie couldn't seem to sit still. "I was there on a misunderstanding. The judge didn't know that—"

"Forget the bullshit." I leaned forward. "Tell me about Dunn or I'll help Derwood work you over."

"Okay, okay," Eddie whined. "Dunn came in, waiting for trial on a home invasion and armed robbery beef. I guess he ripped off some big dealer in Manchester. The minute he came in the joint, half the people there already knew who he was. The other half heard what I heard—that Butchy was a bank robber from Charlestown. He's a legend down in the projects there. He's got his own gang of Irish thugs that worship him. My cellie told me that he heard the Mafia in Boston sent one of their top enforcers over to Charlestown to talk to Butchy about paying tribute on all his scores and drug dealing. The next day . . ." Eddie swallowed hard before continuing, "the guineas found their guy's head in a bowling ball bag in front of their North End headquarters. To this day, Dunn's gang is the only gang around that don't kick a tribute up to Boston." Eddie said the last sentence as if he were talking about a religious miracle.

This was worse than I thought. Billy—or Butchy Dunn, as he was apparently known—was no one to fool with. At least I knew why Monica had been so evasive about her brother. She was afraid that I'd be scared off. And maybe she was right. We'd see.

"Anything else?" I asked.

"Just that it took him less than twenty-four hours to become top man in the joint," Eddie said.

"How'd he do that?" I asked. "His reputation?"

"Even worse," Eddie answered. "I guess he was unhappy that there might be a few people who hadn't heard of him, 'cause the next day they found this giant short-caller, Leroy, all fucked up in his cell. Butchy'd beaten him half to death with a sock full of nuts and bolts stolen from the prison workshop."

"Did he die?" I asked.

Eddie gulped. "No, if you can call wearin' a diaper and droolin' like an idiot for the rest of your life, living."

I fought to get the images of Leroy-with-the-bashed-in-head out of my mind. My heart thumped louder than a drummer on a roll. "Why'd Dunn look you up here on the beach?"

"Tell Dan the truth, Eddie," Derwood said, rolling his eyes. Before Eddie could speak, Derwood turned to me. "Eddie was Butchy's little bitch while he was in jail. He was doin' Butchy's laundry and all his errands. If he was in there any longer, Butchy would have had Eddie wearin' a dress and lipstick."

"Very funny, Dumwood," Eddie said, his cheeks burning red.

"I warned you, Eddie. Don't call me that." Derwood reached over and poked his thick forefinger directly into the dark blue eggplant-shaped bulge under Eddie's eye. Eddie howled like a cat caught by a pit bull. When Derwood removed his finger, there was a white print on the purple bruise. Tears rolled from Eddie's swollen eye.

I almost felt bad for him. If it'd been someone else, I might have. For Eddie Hoar, no.

"He musta been braggin' to Butchy," Derwood continued, "that he was some big shot around here. Butchy remembered that when he got out on parole."

I struggled to get the new vision—Eddie all dolled up in makeup and a dress—out of my head. "So your mouth got you in trouble again, huh, Eddie?"

"His big mouth has gotten us all in trouble," Derwood said, shaking his head. "That's for sure."

"And what's he want with me again?" I asked, glaring at Eddie.

The words came out in a rush. "He wants to know about some money you and his sister are looking for. That's what he wants, Dan. Some buried money. Fifteen grand, I think he said. And you gotta tell him what you know. When he finds out Derwood and me didn't find anything at your place . . . he'll . . . he'll . . ."

"Forget it," I interrupted. "I get the picture." And I did. I couldn't really blame Eddie and Derwood for breaking into my house. Not after being threatened by a maniac like Butchy Dunn. I might have followed his orders, too.

Still, I was curious about one thing—why would a hardcore criminal like Dunn be so hot to get his hands on fifteen thousand dollars? Sure, it was nothing to sneeze at for most people, but I had to believe that a tough guy like Butchy Dunn had access to all sorts of illegitimate cash streams from armed robberies, shakedowns, drug dealings, and who knew what else. Would he really involve himself in a small-potatoes score or would he send an underling to handle it? Especially when on parole.

And what about his sister? Why didn't he let his sister have the fifteen thousand? Even an animal like Dunn usually had strong family and neighborhood ties.

Eddie'd said Billy was a legend in the Charlestown projects. The area was famous for its Code of Silence. Those who lived there were referred to as Townies if I remembered right. The term 'thick as thieves' might have been coined on the streets around Bunker Hill, for all I knew.

You didn't become a legend in a place like that by screwing your flesh and blood out of a measly fifteen thousand bucks. Something wasn't right. And telling Eddie about it was a foolish move. Butchy sounded anything but foolish.

I wrapped up my conversation with Eddie and Derwood, convincing them I'd help as best I could. I told Eddie to string Butchy along, assure him I was about to give Eddie the info he was looking for. I hoped that would keep all of us—Shamrock, Dianne, myself, and even Eddie and Derwood—out of harm's way while I figured out what I was going to do next.

Chapter 11

AFTER MY CONVERSATION with Eddie and Derwood I went to the High Tide for my shift. I got the bar all set up, then opened the front door for another day in paradise.

Of course, Eli and Paulie entered almost immediately and took their customary stools, Eli opposite the beer spigots and Paulie at the far end. They'd been silently nursing their first beers for less than ten minutes when a man walked through the door.

I didn't need to check his ID to know who he was. Taller than my five foot nine and solid muscle. Black, short-sleeve jersey stretched across a rock-hard chest and bulging biceps, likely a benefit of spending prison time lifting weights. Tight, black designer jeans and what looked like expensive white sneakers completed the ensemble.

Butchy Dunn.

My anxiety level rose faster than an express elevator as he stopped and took in the scene. Eli and Paulie glanced at the man and quickly looked away. I took it for granted they had no idea who this guy was, just that he was a threatening presence. If they'd known his identity, I was sure they would have gulped their beer and made a hasty exit.

Behind Dunn lurked an Irish thug if there ever was one. The man was huge—at least six foot four and two hundred fifty pounds. He wore a green sweatshirt with the word SOUTHIE printed on the front. His face looked like that of an ex-prize fighter who'd lost more bouts than he'd won. He had a cauliflower ear the size of a large fist. On his huge, pumpkin-size head was a too-small scally cap, white with a green shamrock on it. The cap looked comical on the huge head, though I doubted anyone ever laughed in his face.

Butchy walked up to where Eli was sitting and stood behind him. I could see Eli's eyelids open like slow-rising window shades. Just when it looked like he couldn't open his eyes any wider, Butchy growled, "Get the fuck down the other end."

I was surprised how fast Eli could move for a man who rarely went any farther than his stool to the men's room and back again. He moved so fast his beer came dangerously close to sloshing out of its mug as he made a beeline to a stool beside Paulie.

I polished already spotless glasses as Butchy mounted the stool Eli had vacated. His bodyguard stood behind him, unmoving.

"What can I get you?" I asked, grateful to hear my voice staying steady.

"Soda water," Butchy said.

I stole furtive glances at my visitor as I poured his drink. His forearms, resting on the bar, sported crude tattoos so faded I couldn't make out what they were. Cheap prison design, I figured. His hair was jet black and combed straight back on his head with a widow's peak. A close-cropped beard partially covered a thin scar that ran from his right cheekbone down under the beard. His nose was just a bit out of line. Even with all this, he was what some women might have called 'bad-boy handsome.'

When I set the drink down in front of him, he said nothing. "Would you like a menu?" I asked, feeling the fool.

Butchy grunted, then glanced toward Eli and Paulie sitting silently at their end of the bar, both staring down at their beers. I would've been doing the same—or been long gone. Maybe their curiosity outweighed the feeling of danger. Or maybe they were just too scared to move.

"Forget the small talk, Marlowe," Dunn said. He'd lowered his voice, but somehow that made the words even more menacing. "You know who I am?"

I nodded, rubbing the dishrag around a glass clutched tightly in my other hand. I was lucky the glass hadn't shattered.

Dunn took the swizzle straw from his drink and flicked the straw at me. I tried hard not to flinch as the straw bounced off my face. Behind him, Cauliflower snickered. Butchy took a drink, studying me over the glass. Those eyes—they would definitely be tough to lie to.

"What's my sister told you?"

"About what?"

Dunn sprang from his stool and grabbed the front of my shirt, yanking me forward with such force that my forehead cracked against one of the steel beer spigots. I could hear Cauliflower snicker again even though I was more than a bit dazed.

"Don't fuck with me, Marlowe." Dunn shoved me backwards, hard. I banged onto the back bar. A few liquor bottles clinked but nothing fell or broke.

I looked at Dunn; he looked back. I resisted touching my forehead until blood ran into my eye. I'd held onto the glass and the cloth I'd been using to wear it out with. I set the glass down on the backbar and dabbed blood from around my eye and forehead with the cloth. Dunn looked like all he'd done was shake my hand.

Eli and Paulie were transfixed by their beers. They both probably wished they'd left when they had the chance. Too late now.

"Come here," Butchy said. He sat on the stool like he'd done no more than sign his name.

I approached the bar, stopping just out of arm's reach. I dabbed a couple of times more at my forehead. The bleeding seemed to have stopped.

I remembered the Georgia Toothpick under the bar, a Louisville slugger that had been there since I'd first owned the High Tide. More for confidence when ejecting a troublesome drunk than for actual use. I couldn't remember even showing it more than once or twice in all the years I'd been here. I toyed with the idea of grabbing the bat now.

Even though I could be fairly sure Dunn wasn't armed—having nowhere to hide a weapon in his tight-fitting clothes—I'd be a fool if I tried to intimidate him. I certainly had no experience bashing anyone with a baseball bat. Whereas Dunn probably beat heads for recreation.

If I raised the bat, he'd likely take it from me and show me how he'd earned his violent reputation. And he had Cauliflower for backup. The only things that would have put me on an even keel with them right about now were both at my cottage—Betsy, my double-barreled shotgun, and the .38 revolver I kept in my nightstand.

"I'll ask you once more," Dunn said. "What the fuck did she tell you and the Irishman?" The soft-spoken words carried more menace than if they'd been shouted by a giant.

I was ready this time, though. Ready to jump backwards. I was out of his reach, hoping that a mad man like Dunn wouldn't go too far in a public place. Though the witnesses might as well have been dead themselves for all the movement my two other customers made.

"She didn't tell me anything," I answered.

Dunn just stared at me. I wondered if he could hear my heart pounding. If not, he was probably the only person within a mile who couldn't hear the pile driver going off in my chest.

"Okay, smart guy," he finally said. "I guess it's kinda nice you ain't got a big mouth." His eyes narrowed. "But would you have something to tell me if your Mick friend was gonna get hurt? Or better—how about the broad who owns this place? Dianne, right? She's your old lady, ain't she?"

Cauliflower's sneer was evil.

I felt like I was on the ocean in the middle of a hurricane. Eddie must have told Dunn about Dianne. I couldn't really blame Eddie, not after seeing his nasty-looking eye and knowing what a psycho maniac Dunn was. Still, Eddie should have told me that Dunn knew about Dianne. Then again, that was Eddie. He'd probably blabbed so much Dunn had to bitch-slap him to get him to shut up.

Before I could respond, Dunn chuckled, a chilling sound that rose from deep in his throat.

"So that's the way it's gonna be." He pointed his index finger at me—thumb up, gun-style—and pointed directly at my head. "Whatever my sister told you . . . you're gonna tell me. And anything else you know, you're gonna tell me. You ain't tellin' anyone else. You got it, smart ass? Then you're gonna butt outta my business for good and stay away from my sister. Got it, Shit for Brains? If you don't do what I'm tellin' ya, next time we meet it won't be in a place with witnesses. Know what I mean?"

Silence dominated the room, then, "Bang!" Dunn's gun-shaped hand actually recoiled.

So did my head.

"And you two," Butchy said, turning toward Eli and Paulie. "You both heard nothin'. Otherwise, Marlowe's chick's gonna be buying a new plate glass window to replace what's left after I throw you both through that window behind you. Understand?"

Eli nodded more rapidly than the hands of a worker being paid by the piece. Paulie nodded twice.

Butchy Dunn stood up. "I'll see ya later, Marlowe. Come on, Angus. Let's get out of here."

He headed out the front door, followed by Cauliflower, off to do whatever the hell a man like that did to fill his days. I just hoped I'd never find out exactly what that was.

Chapter 12

"IF I WERE ten years younger, I woulda given the punk a good thrashing," Eli said. "Him manhandling Dan like that."

He glared at the front door Butchy Dunn had just passed through. Of course, Eli had reclaimed his stool near the beer spigots the second he was sure Dunn was gone.

Paulie guffawed, rolled his eyes at his drinking partner, and said, "I suppose you would have taken care of his little friend, too. Who do you think you're shitting? You were so scared you couldn't lift your glass without slopping beer all over the place, for Chrissake."

"I didn't see you giving him any lip," Eli said. "And you're a young guy. You shoulda put him in his place."

"Dan doesn't like trouble at the bar," Paulie said. "Do ya, Dan?"

"What?" I'd been thinking of what Butchy Dunn had said, not what Eli and Paulie were rambling about now. "Yeah, yeah. I'll get you another beer."

I got a bottle for Paulie, poured a draft for Eli, and set them down in front of them.

The swinging doors that led from the dining room to the kitchen squeaked. Moments later, Dianne came around the wood partition that separated the bar from the dining room, sparing a quick glance at the stocked aquarium atop the partition. She gave Eli and Paulie a nod and walked up to me at the bar. Her black hair was pulled back as it was every day at work. She wore a white restaurant shirt loose over navy knee-length shorts. She still had an end-of-summer tan that made her green eyes even more attractive. A dishcloth draped casually over her right shoulder.

"Dan, I need to talk to you about rotating the beer in the cooler. You're going to have to remember to take care of that. The night staff just does not have the time."

"Okay, that's no problem," I said. "I won't forget."

Dianne stared at me, her light brows furrowed. "What happened to you?" She pointed a thin finger at my face.

I turned my head and peered in the backbar mirror. A thin line of dried blood traced from the top of my forehead to my eyebrow. I also had a nice welt forming.

"You just missed all the action, Dianne," Eli burst out. "Some crazy man came in and assaulted Dan."

I gave Eli the evil eye. He cleared his throat. "'Course, I'm sure he wouldn't have let him get away with that 'ceptin' he didn't want any damage done to your place."

Dianne looked at Eli like he was six cents short of a nickel. She turned back to me. "What the hell is he talking about?"

I didn't want to get into this with Dianne. Like I said, we were on the outs and it was mostly my fault.

"It was nothing," I said. "Just some jerk who had too much to drink before he came in. I refused to serve him."

She put her hands on her hips, checked out my forehead again. "And he did that to you?"

"Yeah," I said lamely.

Dianne looked quickly at Eli. "Is that true?"

Eli had just taken a sip of beer and he sputtered most of it back into his glass. "Ahh . . . yeah, yeah. Is what true?"

Dianne took two steps over to Eli. "That someone was drunk and punched Dan?"

"Well . . . I . . . ahh, he didn't punch Dan," Eli stumbled. "He cracked his head against this here beer thingy." He reached out and jiggled the spigot my head had been banged against.

"What?" Dianne stared hard at Eli. "You're trying to tell me a drunk comes in here at eleven in the morning and slams Dan's head against the beer spigot? Just because he was re-fused service?"

Eli looked desperately at me, then turned toward Paulie down at the end of the bar, and back at me again. I shook my head slightly. Dianne caught the movement and jumped on Eli. "Don't look at him. Tell me what happened."

"He . . . he . . . he was defending you," Eli said, looking at Dianne. "The guy made some threatenin' remarks about you and the Irishman."

I interrupted. "He just had you confused with someone else."

Too little, too late. Dianne turned on me. "What are you mixed up in now?"

Before I could answer, her green eyes flashed. "And if you've got me or the restaurant involved in anything, I'll . . . I'll . . ."

Dianne spun and headed back the way she'd come, al-most banging into Shamrock who was coming around the partition. He stumbled out of her way and came up to the bar.

"What the hell's the matter with her?" he asked.

"This tough guy—" Eli started.

I interrupted again. "Drop it, Eli."

He did. He knew I wasn't fooling. I was already on thin ice with Dianne, and Eli had just melted said ice another inch or two.

"You never know when to keep your trap shut, old man," Paulie said.

"My trap shut? Listen you, I'll have you know I . . ."

While Paulie and Eli went at each other, I motioned for Shamrock to follow me to the far end of the bar, out of ear-shot of my two customers. We leaned in close to each other across the bar.

"It was Monica's brother, Billy. 'Butchy' Dunn," I said in a low voice.

Shamrock's eyes grew large. "Dunn? Here? What the hell did he want?"

"He wants to know what his sister told us. Along with anything else we know."

"But we don't know nothing . . . or almost nothing. Did you tell him that?"

"Of course, I did. He thinks I'm lying."

Shamrock pointed a scarred index finger at my head. "He do that?"

I nodded. "He threatened you, too, Shamrock."

My friend's Adam's apple slid up and down. "Me?"

"Yeah, you and Dianne."

"Dianne?" Shamrock said, his voice hitting a high note. "She doesn't know anything."

"Leverage against me, I guess," I said.

"Is that why she went out of here like a wench on fire?"

I nodded.

"You told her about Dunn?" Shamrock looked at me like I was wearing a dunce cap. "You told her about him?"

I turned my head and looked down the bar.

"Eli!" Shamrock snorted. "This is bad, Danny. Dianne'll really be on the warpath now. And I just about had her convinced you were a member of the human race."

"This isn't funny, Shamrock. Dunn's no one to fool with. I know that now. He's made threats against all three of us."

"Jesus, son of sweet Mother Mary." Shamrock used one hand to rub his face hard. "I'll go talk to her, try to calm her down." He started to leave, hesitated, and added, "I don't like this, Danny. Not much scares me . . . but this? Butchy Dunn? I don't know. Maybe we ought to cut out of this. A few thousand dollars ain't worth tanglin' with the likes of him." He paused. "Of course, it's Dianne I'm thinkin' of. Christ, anything happened to her . . . I . . . I . . ."

He didn't finish his thought. And it didn't matter. I had enough thoughts for both of us. I was in love with Dianne, and Shamrock thought of her as a sister. So Dunn's threat against her had thrown us both. But there was one thought that kept popping up and pushing out the rest.

All this was over fifteen thousand crummy bucks?

The smart thing would be to let Dunn have it. But what about his sister, Monica? I'd made a deal. I didn't like to break my word. But what I'd like even less would be for any harm to come to my best friend and my . . . my . . . to Dianne.

Chapter 13

"DANIEL, OH DANIEL. Could you come up here for a minute?"

I'd just left my shift at the High Tide and was only yards away from my place when I heard the shaky, bird-like voice of my neighbor, Cora Petit. She had her hands on the railing of her front porch as she called to me. I climbed the peeling porch stairs and plunked down in a rocker beside the one she was slowly lowering herself into.

It was a brisk late September day, autumn-like, but not cold. Still, Cora wore black wool slacks, a white sweater over a light pink blouse with a high collar, and a heavy, long, rainbow-colored shawl wrapped snuggly around her shoulders and folded down to her lap. When she was seated comfortably, we exchanged pleasantries.

Finally, Cora said, "I just wanted to tell you that I talked to my friend, Gertrude Mahoney. You know Gertrude, don't you, Daniel?"

I didn't know Gertrude personally, but I did know she was an elderly lady who lived around the corner on River Street. She was probably in her late eighties, had been around the beach forever, and was a crony of Cora's. "I know who she is."

"Well . . ." Cora began. "I spoke to her about the camps that were here back in the old days. My memory isn't what it used to be, like I told you, and I just wanted to make sure I remembered correctly. I was close. Her memory is so very good. She said the camp that was here before this one," Cora pointed a gnarled finger toward the cottage beside hers, "was so badly damaged in the hurricane of 1938 that it had to be torn down. I asked her if the cottage could have been called 'Seaview.' She couldn't be sure but said it did ring a bell. Neither of us are sure about it, though. There were so many repairs and whatnot going on after those big storms, especially that one."

"Oh." I swallowed a sigh. When Cora had called me to join her, I'd hoped she had some new nugget of information, information that would propel me forward in my search. I was half right. It was info, but how good that information was wasn't apparent.

"You look disappointed, Daniel. You shouldn't be. At least you have an idea what this street looked like back then. You won't have to go over to the Lane Library to do research." She hesitated, her eyes sparkling hopefully. "Are you writing a book by any chance? I'd love to read a good book about the history of our beach."

I didn't have the heart to put the kibosh on her little dream, though why anyone would think I could write a book was beyond me. "Maybe some day, but for right now I'm just satisfying my curiosity."

She clasped her hands—still holding the shawl—in front of her as though praying in church. "Oh, my goodness, a book about our beach would be just wonderful. There is so much history here."

If that wasn't an opening, nothing was. Maybe I could get another kernel of useful information out of this visit with Cora. I'd have to be discreet, though. Yes, she was a little old lady sitting on a porch, but who knew how many people she spoke to during the course of a week? I still wanted to keep the possibility of gold here quiet.

"Have you ever heard of any smuggling on Hampton Beach?" I finally asked.

"Oh, my," she said, her eyes widening. "You mean the boat with the drugs and poor dead souls on it that crashed into the jetty?"

Good grief—not again. I was still trying to forget that incident, the incident that had ended up sucking me and Shamrock into a nightmare that almost ended with the two of us having our tickets punched—permanently.

"No, Cora, not that. I was thinking . . ." I cleared my throat. "About liquor smuggling. Along the beach. Back during Prohibition."

Cora raised her thin shoulders. She was a teetotaler, I was sure, and for a minute I thought I might have offended her by even mentioning the subject.

"Liquor was never talked about when I was a young girl, Daniel."

My collar suddenly felt tight.

"Not in front of my mother, at least. Emile did like a nip now and then, though." She was referring to her father. Her shoulders relaxed. "Can I tell you a story in strict confidence, Daniel?" She reached out and touched my bare arm with icy-cold fingers.

"Of course, you can." And I meant it.

She shuddered as she removed her hand from my arm and pulled the shawl tighter around her tiny shoulders.

"Well, Emile," she began, her smooth cheeks turning red, "my father, did like a taste now and then, as I said. I don't remember how old I was . . . a young girl, though. In this very house, I was awoken in the dead of night by an awful howling and a thumping noise. Terrified, I climbed from my bed and went down the hallway. The noise was coming from my parents' room. I peeked in and . . . as I said, I was a young girl and my mother and father loved each other. I had no idea what was happening until . . . I saw . . ."

Cora was trying to catch her breath.

"Are you all right, Cora?"

"Yes . . . yes . . . I'm . . . fine." After a long moment, she composed herself and continued. "It's almost funny now. But you have to remember . . . I was very young, and I had never seen either my mother or father ever raise a hand to the other. And there Mother was, swinging a broom and beating a large form on the bed. The form was wrapped in a blanket and tied up with thick twine. After a few seconds, I realized the lump was my father, and every time the broom crashed into him, he let out a terrible howl.

"'You wicked man,' Mother yelled. 'I warned you that if you ever came home drunk again, this is what you'd get. This time you weren't just drunk . . . you were stinko drunk. You didn't even open a blood-shot eye as I tied you up in your puke-covered blanket. Animal! This'll teach you.'"

"Wow," I said as Cora took a breath.

"Yes," Cora said. "I could hear every word Mother said, even though she was probably trying to keep her voice low.

There was more Mother said, but I'd rather not repeat it. After a bit, I went back to my room."

"What happened after that?" I asked.

Cora smiled. "Nothing. I never told my parents I'd heard anything. The incident was never mentioned in the family. My father never drank again, though, as far as I know."

"I can't blame him. Your mother must have been a real spitfire."

"She was a fine woman, Daniel. French stock. Would cut off her arm for a family member. But she wouldn't put up with any tomfoolery either."

"I guess not." It was a great story, but it had nothing to do with what I'd hoped to hear.

Chapter 14

I WAS ABOUT to excuse myself when Cora said, "You know, Daniel, there is one person you may want to talk to."

"Who's that?"

"Albert Keel."

"I don't think I know him."

She shook her head so hard I was afraid her frail neck might break. "No, you wouldn't. He's not a beach person. From Manchester, although he calls a nursing home over in Exeter his home now."

Manchester, about forty miles away, was New Hampshire's largest city. Exeter was a town adjacent to Hampton. I was curious to see where this was leading.

"You would like him," Cora continued. "The stories that man can tell. I used to be in a little group that visited the residents in nursing homes. I can't do it anymore. Takes too much out of me. And, God forbid, if I end up in one of those places, I think I'd—"

I interrupted. "What kinds of stories, Cora?"

Cora waved a hand. "Fantastic stories. Some about our beautiful seacoast. The man can talk."

"But what about?" I asked.

"Prohibition. Smuggling. What you asked about. And he loves visitors. He's smart as a whip, but the poor man is bedridden and stuck in that place." Cora shivered.

I was growing a bit excited but was also confused. "How does he know these stories?"

"He was a United States Treasury agent. If he said that once, he said it a million times, every time my group paid him a visit. Worked for the Prohibition Bureau. An Alcohol man. I don't think Father would have liked him. Mother would have, though."

If anyone knew what had really happened on Hampton Beach so many decades ago, this man might.

"Do you think I might speak with him?" I asked.

Cora beamed. "Of course, Daniel, as long as he's still able. As I said, the man loves visitors. And the staff encourages people to come read, chat, play cards, and things like that with the patients, especially if they have no family."

"Could you arrange for me to see him?"

"I'll call Gertrude. I think she still visits him occasionally."

We talked for a bit more. I don't think there was anything else of significance said, but I probably wouldn't have remembered anyway. My mind was off in a nursing home room, chatting with an old Prohibition agent with a barrelful of stories to tell.

Chapter 15

THE ELMWOOD NURSING Facility was a white one-story stone building in Exeter. The grounds were impeccably landscaped. I hoped the inside was half as well cared for.

I drove my green Chevette into the lot at the side of the building and parked in a spot marked for visitors. I made my way up the winding concrete path that led to double-glass front doors, walked in, and presented myself at the front desk.

A harried-looking woman stood behind the counter, fingers playing piano on the countertop while her eyes danced about, landing on everything but me. I explained who I was there to see and she directed me to a room.

I was almost halfway down the corridor when an elderly woman in a wheelchair spoke to me. I couldn't catch exactly what she said, so I stepped closer. Her arm shot out like an arrow from a bow. A hand, bulged with thick blue veins and wrinkles as numerous as a slept-in shirt after a three-day bender, seized my arm and clamped hard on it.

"I knew you'd come! I knew you'd come! I knew you'd come!" Her eyes were wide and frantic. I tried to calm her with soothing words, but it was useless. Her grip on my arm only tightened. I tried to pull my arm free but she wouldn't let go. I didn't want to tip her wheelchair over. I looked both ways along the corridor—no help in sight.

One by one, I grabbed her fingers and struggled to bend them backwards, praying her fingers wouldn't snap like dried twigs. Her frantic expression never changed, nor did she give up the pitiful chant.

Finally, in desperation, I said, "I'm here," and wrapped my free hand around three of her fingers and gently pulled them backward without hurting her. I could feel her relax and her grip loosened enough that I was able to tear my arm free.

I jumped out of reach and hurried along the side of the corridor in the direction I'd been heading before being hijacked by the confused woman in a wheelchair. I vowed silently to myself to choose Smith & Wesson over Elmwood, or a similar facility if it ever came to that.

I tried to shake off the encounter as I approached the room I wanted. The door was open; I stepped inside.

Two side-by-side beds faced two other beds, a rolling tray table beside each. Windows dominated the far wall. The other walls were painted lettuce green. On the right, two neatly made beds sat empty. On the left, the bed near the window was messy and empty, but the bed closest to me was occupied. I could see movement under the thin blanket. Albert Keel—or so I assumed—the man I had come to see. He was obviously awake.

I walked over to the bed. "Mr. Keel? I'm Dan Marlowe. Gertrude Mahoney may have told you I was coming?"

"Of course, she did," Albert Keel said. "Have a seat."

He threw the blanket off his body. I dragged a blue, vinyl-covered chair closer to the bed and sat down.

"It's nice to meet you," I said, extending my hand.

"Good to meet you, too." He didn't raise his arm off the bed. Like a dunce I left my hand suspended in midair for a short minute before I realized the man was blind. I put my hand in my lap. His watery blue eyes stared hard, but not at me. Behind me.

Albert Keel raised his frail body higher on a pillow that cushioned his back from the headboard. "Gertrude told me you're writing a book, huh? About Prohibition? Smugglers? Well, you've come to the right place. Dan, right?"

I decided to ignore the book comment. Otherwise, I'd have to come up with another reason for my interest. "Yes, Mr. Keel. And yes, it's Dan."

I took note of his lack of hair. I don't mean that this man was just bald on his head. He sported no hair anywhere I could see. Besides the completely barren top of his head, he was lacking any facial hair and didn't look like he needed to shave in the morning. I was envious of that. He had no eyebrows or any hair on his arms. I assumed his whole body must be that way. Medication, possibly.

"Forget the Mister . . . it's Albert." His gaze shifted toward the ceiling, and for a moment I had the odd feeling he'd regained his sight. "They used to call me Agent Keel back in the rum-running days. The days you're interested in, right?"

"Yes. It must have been an exciting job."

"Oh, boy, you don't know the half of it. But I'm going tell you what you missed. Hampton Beach. Gertie said you're from Hampton Beach, right?"

"Yes," I answered.

"Have I got stories about that place."

This was starting out better than I'd hoped. I'd been afraid I'd have to pump a dementia-plagued old man to remember events more than a half century ago. Cora had been right—this man's brain was as sharp as a damn tack, no matter how ravaged his body was.

"I'm a bartender on Hampton Beach."

"A bartender! Christ, back in the day I would have been shutting you down, my boy." He leaned forward and waved his arm around until his hand found my knee and gave it a reassuring shake. "Only kidding, Dan. We didn't bother with speaks and such, especially ones out in the boonies. No, we went after the big boys—the syndicates, the smugglers, the king pins. That's where the action was."

His puny chest inflated. "And Hampton Beach?" He let out a cackle. "We used to call it Hooch Beach. There was more booze brought in there than into an Irish wake. The Isles of Shoals, too. You know the place? A few small islands about a dozen miles out?"

I nodded, then remembered he couldn't see. "Yes."

I barely got the word out before he continued. "Lots of times, if the weather was rough or they thought we were waiting for them on Hooch Beach or in the harbor, they'd get cute and drop the booze out there. Pick up the sauce and bring it ashore later when things cooled down. And pick up the gold."

For the next fifteen minutes or so, I barely spoke a word. Agent Keel told a story that was like an adventure tale. No, it was an adventure tale. A true adventure tale. I felt like I was a little boy again, back in my bedroom, my mother reading pages from *Treasure Island* to me every night. She was the one sitting in a chair back then; I was in my bed. For the first time in a long time, I felt the same excitement I had felt all those years ago.

"You mentioned gold." I said. "Why gold?"

"The market crash in '29," he said. "The smugglers didn't trust the greenback anymore. And who could blame them? More banks were closing than livery stables when I was a kid, horses on the way out and cars coming in. It was damn frightening, I'll tell you. Banks were going under faster than residents in this hell hole." He turned and looked at the empty bed across from him.

"So, the smugglers wanted to be paid in gold?"

"That's right. Gold and nothing but."

A thought I'd had earlier popped up again. "How did the bootleggers get gold to pay with?"

Albert chuckled. "Back then we had a lot of gold coins in circulation. That was before FDR called them all in, 1933 or so. That's all the smugglers would take were them gold coins. Especially the gangs out of Saint Pierre. The biggest smuggling ring was run by a combo headed by Joe Kennedy, King Solomon from Boston, and a couple of big New Hampshire names. They didn't do any loads of less than twenty-five grand."

"Saint Pierre?"

"Yeah, Saint Pierre. Solomon's gang was plugged in with the Frenchies up there," Keel answered. "Still don't understand why they don't teach that in geography classes here. It's an island off the coast of Newfoundland. French. Still is. Only land the French ended up with in North America. More booze entered the east coast of the United States from Saint Pierre than Canada or the Caribbean combined.

Those damn frogs had their shit together, as the kids say. We couldn't touch them up there, being part of France. And they were too far away from their homeland for France to clamp down on them, like Canada did a bit on Seagram and those assholes."

"I never heard about the place," I admitted.

"Most people haven't," Albert said. "Little known fact. That and the gold. The smugglers that worked out of there wanted to be paid in twenty-dollar coins. Most in circulation back then were Saint Gaudens, double eagles with a Standing Lady Liberty on the face. Beautiful coin. Lots in circulation back then. Probably worth plenty today."

"Do you remember a state cop getting killed in a shoot-out with bootleggers in Hampton, back in 1930?" I asked.

"Of course I do," he said, raising his voice. Then he lowered his voice and added, "But I missed out on that action. Assigned elsewhere at the time."

He told me what he knew of the incident, which wasn't much more than I already knew. He seemed genuinely disappointed that he'd missed the firefight.

Albert Keel continued with his adventure tales, but now it seemed he was rehashing the same memories—or maybe I was just distracted by gold coins and a French island called Saint Pierre. Something that didn't fit with what else I knew.

Finally, he turned his watery eyes toward me. "Have you run into Capo—?"

A nurse bustled in. She said in a Jamaican lilt, "Mister Keel, it is time for your sponge bath."

Time for me to go. I got up, took Agent Keel's hand in mine, and genuinely thanked him for the visit. He said I could come back anytime if I wanted more information for the book. His voice seemed filled with hope. I didn't like this place. I did like the man, though. Very much.

As I headed down the corridor, I saw the old woman who had nearly broken my arm. She was seated exactly where she had been before, against one wall. I clung to the opposite wall as I passed. She reached for me, again chanting, "I knew you'd come . . . I knew you'd come . . . I knew you'd come . . ."

I was glad to get out of the place. On the ride home, all I could think of were gold coins, the little island of Saint Pierre, and what Agent Keel had started to say before being interrupted for a sponge bath. "Have you run into Capo—"

The only capo I'd ever heard of was the term used for a mafia street crew boss. Didn't I already have my hands full with an infamous Irish thug from Charlestown, Massachusetts?

I shuddered and turned my thoughts back to the saints— twenty-dollar Saint Gaudens gold coins and the French Island of Saint Pierre.

Chapter 16

"AGAIN?" MY IRISH friend asked.

"Yes, again," I answered.

We were back in my green Chevette and had just crossed over the Hampton Bridge on our way to Seabrook. There was something I wanted to check out. Albert Keel had said, "They're probably worth plenty today," referring to the gold coins. I wanted to see what exactly 'plenty' meant. If he was right, it would make sense out of a couple things that troubled me, including why a big-time gangster like Butchy Dunn was so hot to trot for this cache of coins. Even though Albert had said the smugglers never did less than $25,000 loads, I still wasn't sure even that amount would be enough to cause Dunn to run amok on the beach.

"Seabrook," Shamrock said. "We always seem to end up over there. And this time for coins. You said the old cop told you about the . . . the . . . what were they?"

"Double eagles. Saint Gaudens. Twenty-dollar gold pieces."

"All righty then, Danny. You know that's what we're look-ing for and that they might be buried on the beach some-where. Why the trip then? I don't like Seabrook."

"What's wrong with Seabrook? A lot of customers from Seabrook come to the Tide. I don't understand why you don't like it."

"Because Seabrook reminds me of those two eejits, Hoar and Doller. And that horrible power plant."

"What about that dirty bookstore with the live models? You like that plenty." I glanced quickly at my companion. His cheeks flushed.

"That was just a couple of times. I haven't visited there in quite a while."

"I heard you were on a first-name basis with every girl over there."

"Ha, ha, Danny, very funny. Keep your eyes on the road."

We were both silent the rest of the short trip. It wasn't long before I pulled into a small strip mall parking lot off Route 1. A stand-alone, one-story wooden building sat directly in front of me. I stopped short of the few parking spots that abutted the front of the fire-engine red building and stared.

"Buffalo Nickels Numis . . . num . . . istics." Shamrock was struggling to decipher the large sign on the front of the building.

"Numismatics," I said. "Means the hobby of coin collecting."

"I know, but why they gotta use a tongue twister like that? Not good business."

Maybe. Maybe not. But that wasn't why I was here. I pulled the car into a parking slot close to the door. I didn't see anyone around, and I wondered for a moment if they were open. Unlikely they'd be closed at noon on a weekday. I hoped I was right.

Shamrock and I got out of the car and marched up to the front door. The door was one of those jobs with very thick glass that ran from top to bottom. I could see wire security threads in the glass. On the inside of the door facing out was the depiction of a large buffalo head, a buffalo nickel, I assumed. A nickel the size of a large pizza box.

I tried the door; it was locked. I gave the handle a little jiggle. Nothing.

"Great," said Shamrock.

I cupped my hands over my eyes and peered through the glass window. I could see someone behind a counter perusing a newspaper at the far end of the store. I was just about ready to give the door a good beating when I saw a red door bell off to the side, RING TO ENTER stenciled below it. I jabbed the bell more than once.

The newspaper reader got up and strolled to the door. He eyeballed Shamrock and me, looking us both up and down. When he was apparently assured we weren't a couple of armed robbers out for a score, he unlocked the door. He held the door open while Shamrock and I squeezed past him, then quickly locked it behind us.

"Come on up here, gents," he said as he passed us and led the way to the counter where I'd first seen him sitting. He walked behind the counter, turned, and faced us.

I hadn't taken note of how tall he was when he first let us in. Standing there in front of me now, I pegged him to be at least six foot four, maybe more. Thin as a rail with a face to match. His ears were pointed like some dogs, and his black haircut was short, a bad chop job if I'd ever seen one. Worse than Derwood Doller's, and that was saying something. He extended his arms, hands splayed on top of the glass display counter. His fingernails were bitten down to the quick. Nerves, I knew. I suffered the same affliction.

"A lot of security," I said.

"Insurance company demands it," he said. "Junkies and stickup men take a liking to these places more than drug stores." He shook his head. "Sorry for the inconvenience. Now, what can I do for you?"

I eyeballed the display case in front of me. Lots of coins, but I had no idea what I was looking at. "I'm interested in gold coins."

One of his eyebrows rose just a bit. "Got plenty. What kind?"

"Double eagles," I said.

His other eyebrow jumped up to join the first.

"What kind of double eagle?" His tone told me he was doubting his decision to let us through the door.

"Saint Gaudens," I answered.

"1920s I'll bet," he said, furrowing his brows. For some reason the furrowed brows made an unnerving combo with his dog-like ears.

"Yes. Why?"

"Because someone else was just in, asking about the double eagles. And the 1920s especially." He gave me the look store owners usually reserved for potential shoplifters.

After a very long, very uncomfortable fraction of a minute, his thin face softened. "Just coincidence, I guess. Don't get much call for that particular coin. Come on over here."

He rounded the counter and walked between the rows of glass display cases all filled with collectible coins.

Shamrock and I fell in behind him. I would've loved to find out who had asked about the twenty-dollar gold coins, but I didn't think it wise. Too many people already knew about the so-called treasure on Hampton Beach. There was me, Shamrock, Dianne, Monica Nichols, Butchy Dunn, Eddie Hoar, Derwood Doller, and who knew who else? I already had an unpleasant idea who'd been asking and I couldn't risk arousing the shop owner's suspicions about what we were up to. I didn't want to get this guy more curious than he already was.

"Here are some beautiful specimens, right here. They each weigh one ounce. So, in today's market, they are worth four hundred dollars each in gold alone."

That got even my ears to stand up. Shamrock and I shared a quick glance.

Dog Ears had one hand on the top of a display case. He bent over to point at some coins on the top shelf, rattling on about the history of the Saint Gaudens twenty-dollar double eagles.

I didn't pay attention to a word he said. I studied the beautiful gold pieces laid out in front of me. Shamrock stood so close his bony shoulder pressed into mine. I could smell the cigarettes on his breath as he studied the coins as closely as I did.

The coins were encased tightly in individual coin holders with round, clear plastic areas that exposed the entire front and back of the coins. Each were minted in various years. My gaze fixated on the small price tags attached to the coins.

Shamrock must have noticed, too. He hit my shoulder twice. "For the love a Jesus, Danny," he whispered. "Look at those prices."

A lot of things were making sense that hadn't before I'd walked into this coin shop.

"I can drag a few out if you have serious interest."

Dog Ears' voice snapped me out of my thoughts. Shamrock and I straightened.

I shook my head. "A little too rich for my blood. They all seem to be around a grand each. That's a lot of money."

Dog Ears shrugged, adding another inch or two to his already formidable height. "Not for the grades I carry," he said as if I'd insulted him. "All at least EF . . ."

He must have picked up on my ignorance. "Extremely Fine condition. I have some rare dates and mint marks, too. They didn't mint that many of them."

"Do you have any brochures on these coins?" I asked.

"No brochures," he answered wearily. "But follow me." He sounded like a man who'd just realized he wasn't going to be making any thousand-dollar sales.

We followed him back to the counter and he handed me a book he picked up from a pile of similar books resting on the counter. It was a red hardcover. The front, embossed in gold, read:

A GUIDEBOOK OF UNITED STATES COINS
48TH EDITION, 1995
R. S. YEOMAN

"All you want to know about the double eagles is in here," Dog Ears said. "Along with information about every other U.S. coin ever minted. The cheap ones as well as the expensive ones."

I didn't like his tone, but I didn't really care enough to respond. I'd found out what I'd wanted to know—the coins were worth a lot more than twenty dollars in today's rare coin market!

I felt I'd finally stumbled across some info of value.

I gave Dog Ears a ten-dollar bill. I took my change and the book. Shamrock and I said goodbye and made a hasty retreat.

We made it onto Route One before Shamrock said, "Holy sweet baby Jesus, Danny! Do you know what this means?"

Yes, I did, but I let Shamrock have the pleasure of saying it out loud.

"Those gold coins, my boy. If that's what Monica and her crazy-ass brother are looking for . . . Danny . . . Jesus . . . they're not worth twenty dollars each anymore. They're worth even better than the pure gold price of four hundred he mentioned. They're worth maybe a thousand dollars apiece to collectors. A thousand dollars. A thousand dollars each. Do you hear me?" Shamrock reached over and shook my arm. Not enough to cause an accident but enough to get my attention. It wasn't necessary, though. The subject already had my full attention.

"I hear you, Shamrock."

Both of us were silent on the way back to Hampton Beach. My brain—and Shamrock's, too—had turned into a temporary calculator trying to figure out how much $25,000 worth of 1920s Saint Gaudens twenty-dollar gold pieces would be worth today.

Chapter 17

IT WAS TIME to see Monica again. I dropped Shamrock off at his place and drove the short distance around Ocean Boulevard and along Ashworth to the Sea Urchin Motel. Fortunately, she was there and let me in after my first knock.

"You've found out something?" She looked at me hopefully. Her blue eyes matched the baby-blue blouse she wore. Her legs were covered, this time in worn jeans that clung to her like plastic wrap.

"A couple of things."

"Tell me."

"Have you had lunch?" I asked.

"No."

"Do you like chicken?"

"Not especially."

"You'll like this chicken. Come on. Where's Sam?"

"He's with my sister."

"Your sister?"

"My sister-in-law," she amended. "My late husband's sister. I trust her with my life. She's not afraid of guns like me. Has a few of her own and she's not afraid to use them. Billy knows that. She grew up in the projects and is tough as nails. Billy would never go near her. She'd shoot him in a heartbeat, believe me."

If half of what Monica said about her was true, Sam was safe. For now.

"If anything ever happens to me," she continued. "I want Sam to live with her. I had a lawyer draw up the papers. Please remember that."

I nodded. "I will."

Monica slipped into a pair of black sneakers. The place I had in mind wasn't too far, so we walked north on Ashworth. The Casino's rear marquee mentioned the names of a few bands I'd never heard of that were wrapping up the ballroom's season. Every summer, I seemed to be less and less familiar with the attractions there. Didn't mean the bands weren't popular. More like it meant I was getting older.

We reached our destination, a small, one-story building kitty-corner with Ashworth and C Street. Monica looked at the sign. "Farr's Famous Chicken. Who's Farr?"

Good question. I shrugged and led the way inside. We found a table, checked out the menu, and ordered.

As the waitress walked away, Monica clutched her hands together and leaned forward. "What have you found out?"

I kept my voice low. "Found out about Butchy Dunn, for one."

"Oh." Her face scrunched. "How?"

"Doesn't matter," I said. "You made your brother seem like Mister Rogers. Now I find out he's a cross between Clyde Barrow and a Mafia hitman."

She reached across the table and put her hand on mine. Her hand was very soft. "I'm sorry, Dan. I was afraid you wouldn't help me if you knew what Billy was like. Don't worry, though. He won't hurt a friend of mine."

"Don't be too sure of that," I said, pointing at the bump on my forehead. "How do you think I got this?"

"Billy," she said, as if she didn't need an answer.

"Yes, your crazy brother almost broke my head open on a beer spigot."

"Dan, I am so sorry."

"Sorry doesn't help, Monica. You should have told me what I was up against."

Monica's hand slid softly across the skin of my hand as she pulled away. "I know. I know. This just means so much to me . . . and to my son." Her eyes misted.

What could I say? I probably would have done the same in her shoes. At least I knew what I was dealing with now.

"I suppose you want to bail out?" she asked.

Before I could answer, our food arrived. After the server left, I said, "No, I'm still in it. For now."

She looked at me like she couldn't believe what I'd just said. I almost couldn't either. But I had a bigger incentive. My twenty-five percent had grown much more attractive now that I knew what we were really looking for. After all, I currently had no money to speak of. I also had children to support.

"Why?" Monica asked.

Instead of answering her question, I asked one of my own. "What else do you know, Monica?"

"What do you mean?"

"About the money? The . . . fifteen thousand dollars," I said with what I hoped was just a taint of sarcasm.

"Just what I told you. It's supposed to be fifteen thousand dollars in gold . . . why?"

I studied her face. If Monica Nichols was lying, she was a very good actress.

Albert Keel had told me the smugglers had never handled loads worth less than twenty-five grand. Maybe Monica had misunderstood her sick grandfather. I was pretty sure she had no idea of the buried gold's true value.

I didn't answer her right away; instead, I began to eat my meal. After a minute, she did, too. We didn't speak again until we were almost done.

"You were right," she said. "It's delicious."

"Told ya."

"Dan?"

I knew she wanted an explanation for my sarcastic question about the money but decided not to tell her. I couldn't be sure she wouldn't tell her brother, although he may have been the one who'd visited the coin store before Shamrock and me. If so, he already knew the treasure's true value. That would explain why an on-parole, big-time gangster would risk violating that parole and why he was so anxious to find said treasure, no matter who got in his way—including his sister and nephew.

On the outside chance he didn't know—being that blood was thicker than water and all—I couldn't risk telling Monica yet.

Though I had to admit to myself, I was beginning to like Monica, crazy brother or not.

"I'm sorry again about Billy. Please be careful. He is dangerous." Her voice shook. I certainly believed her.

"Hopefully we can work around him," I said.

Her eyes grew misty again and then overflowed. "I just want to get Sam out of Charlestown so he doesn't end up like his uncle. Give him a good life. That's all I want."

We finished our meals, left Farr's, and headed back to the Sea Urchin.

Back at Monica's . . . I don't know how it happened. I don't know why it happened. Maybe because I'd told her I was going to stick around even though I knew how danger-ous her brother was. Maybe she looked at me as some type of savior for her son.

I wasn't really surprised when she reached out and took my hands in hers. Surprised? No. Nervous? Yes. I still wasn't sure it wasn't my imagination. Not until she tugged my hands gently toward her. My body followed and pressed against ev-ery inch of her firm body. It had been so damn long. Those full lips of hers felt and tasted so good. I couldn't fight it, even if I'd wanted to. I was hard as a rock, and I just . . . let it happen. And what happened was good . . . awfully good.

Chapter 18

AFTER I LEFT Monica's motel, I headed south along Ashworth Ave on my way home. I felt good. I knew it wouldn't last long . . . that I was sure of. I had some feelings for Monica, but I had stronger feelings for Dianne. But Dianne had dumped me. No guilt there as far as my tumble with Monica went, right?

Who was I kidding? I could already feel guilt creeping into every cell in my stupid brain. If I'd wanted to complicate my life any more than it already was, I couldn't have picked a better way to do it. Getting involved with Butchy Dunn's sister was a stupid move. Especially when I still held out hope of a reconciliation with Dianne.

Shamrock would tear me a new one when he found out. Dianne? I didn't know what she'd do. Could be anything from nothing to tossing me off the cliff at Boar's Head. *If* she found out. I knew then and there I'd do everything I could to prevent that from happening. Like I said, I hadn't given up on us yet. Dianne and me, that is.

Many of the businesses on the beach were closed now that the season was over. Wally's, Hampton Beach's friendliest biker bar, wasn't. I just happened to be across the street from the joint. There were a few people seated at the outside tables, sipping drinks in the afternoon sun. The place would be jumping after dark. I'd spent of lot of time there through the years. Most of it fun. Once or twice, I'd prefer to forget. Not the bar's fault. Mine, of course.

I was still looking across the street when someone stepped out of the doorway of a laundromat and stopped right in front of me. I drew up short to avoid bumping into him. Standing there was one of the weirdest looking characters I'd ever seen on the beach, and believe me, I've seen them all. He was old—eighties, maybe. Tall as me. His cadaverous face sported whiskers only a street bum would dare wear in public.

It was cool out if you can call sixty plus cool, but not so cool anyone would wear the garb this guy had on. He wore a gray wool topcoat buttoned from the throat all the way down to where it ended near his knees. His black wool pants were high-waters that exposed white socks and a badly beaten-up pair of black Florsheim shoes. Perched on his head was one of those old-time soft hats like my father used to wear. A fedora or a porkpie, maybe? I had never gotten the difference straight in my head.

"I want to talk to you, Marlowe," he said in a gravelly voice. A filterless cigarette bobbed between his lips—Pall Mall, Lucky, Camel . . . something like that. The type I thought no one but Eli smoked anymore.

"Who are you?" I asked. I didn't feel threatened, just curious about this person who looked as out of place on Hampton Beach as an Eskimo in summer.

He had both hands in the pockets of his worn overcoat. One hand whipped out holding a leather case, wallet size. He flicked it open, flashed a badge, and—just as quickly—shut it before I could read what I was looking at and returned it to his coat pocket.

"That answer your question, smart guy?" He sneered. The cigarette bobbed, but he didn't take a puff. "I'm the law."

For a moment, I thought I'd walked onto the set of one of those 1940s noir movies that I enjoyed so much.

"What do you want?"

He leaned so close I could see pores the size of manhole covers on his face. "I want you to keep your nose out of other people's business."

I didn't like his breath one bit—combination of foul meat and stale cigarettes.

"Whose business?" I asked.

He pulled his other hand free and pointed his thumb at his chest. "My business and the people's."

"What business? What people?" I asked incredulously.

"You punk," he snarled. "You holding a gat?"

Both his hands snaked out and swiftly patted me down. I was too stunned to stop him.

The odds of this old relic being any kind of cop, except maybe private, were longer than the odds of finding a blue lobster on dry land. But laying a hand on a senior citizen in New Hampshire was a major felony. Better to allow a pat down than the embarrassing publicity and possible prison sentence a tussle with an old man like this could bring on.

When he was satisfied I had no gun, he looked at me with his watery gray eyes. "I know you're playing footsie with the frail, Marlowe."

Frail? I'd never heard the word used to describe a young, good-looking woman—outside of an old hardboiled paperback.

"Don't act dumb. You know what I mean. The Nichols dame," he said coldly. "The gunsel, Butchy Dunn's sister."

Monica and her brother Butchy. I knew that's who he was talking about. But what he was saying about them, I had no idea. "What about them?"

"Don't play me for the sap."

"I won't. If you tell me what you're talking about."

His voice turned even colder and his thin head shook just a bit like he had palsy. "I'd like to have you under a white-hot light for an hour. You wouldn't play dumb then. Especially if I had my persuader." He pretended he was slapping something up and down into his hand, likely imagining he held a blackjack.

I decided to play it cagey with this lunatic. "The girl's just a friend of mine."

"Ha! Some friend. I saw you in the room with her. You should have pulled the shade all the way down."

"So you're a peeping Tom."

"I do what I have to do, Marlowe. To uphold the law." He smiled slyly. "She's a tall glass of water, I'll give ya that. But I know you're in with her. No pun intended. And if you think you're gonna take what's rightfully mine, you got another think coming." His face got hard and he came in close again.

I pulled back.

"Look, I don't know what you're talking about." I could see that some of the patrons at Wally's were looking in our direction.

"Play dumb if you want, Marlowe. Just remember, the cabbage is mine. I've earned it. I'll have the eyeball on ya. So butt out. Fast. Otherwise, I'll put the local bulls on ya and you'll be taking a one-way trip to the big house. Unnerstan?"

No, I didn't 'unnerstan.' But I had no time to tell him that because he turned on his heels and hurried down Ashworth in the direction I'd come. Maybe I should have followed him but I didn't. I was too shocked. Who was this guy? Where had he come from? And what did he want? It was the biggest conundrum I'd run into so far.

Chapter 19

THE NEXT MORNING I was going in the back door of the High Tide and had barely closed the door behind me when Dianne called. "Dan, can you come in for a minute?"

She was seated behind her desk in her small office, the same office that had been mine when I'd owned the Tide. That was back before I'd lost the restaurant—along with my family and any money I'd had at the time—to an all-consuming cocaine habit. I'd finally beaten that habit, notwithstanding a couple of falls off the wagon. Dianne had her black hair pulled back tightly and tied with a green ribbon that matched her eyes. A white restaurant blouse draped loosely over her breasts. She wore little makeup; she didn't need any.

"Close the door and sit down," she said, motioning to the folding chair in front of her desk. I hadn't needed direction on where to sit. It was either the chair or a small dark sofa against the wall.

I sat, feeling a bit guilty. Just yesterday I'd had my romp with Monica Nichols. I wasn't worried that Dianne had found out. Even Hampton Beach's seaweed telegraph wasn't that fast. I was more concerned Dianne would pick up on it the minute she looked at me. She'd known me intimately for a long time. She'd always been able to read me like that damn book they talk about. But maybe my worry was unnecessary. Besides, I wasn't even sure she gave a damn anymore if I was seeing anyone else. Her actions in the recent past seemed to indicate she didn't. Still?

"What the hell happened?" she said, her face pinched.

I thought she meant my time with Monica and was just about to throw myself under the bus, when she added, "Who the hell was that guy and why did he assault you?"

"I told you he was just some drunk."

Her eyes flashed. "You're lying, Dan, I can tell."

She grabbed a letter opener and pointed it in my direction. "Now . . . tell . . . me . . . the . . . truth."

I didn't think she'd use the tiny blade on me, but knowing her fiery disposition, I didn't want to take the chance. Still, I couldn't tell her the true story. Yet.

After a minute, she seemed to cool down. "You're lucky I've put you back on the bar. If it wasn't for your kids, I probably wouldn't have."

This was turning out just as bad as I'd imagined, though in a different direction. "Dianne, I—"

"Shut up," she said, her eyes wild. "I want to know what that scene in the bar was all about," she repeated. "I know you and I know the type of things you get mixed up in."

I stood. "Dianne, I—"

"Don't lie to me," she said before I could. "I have a very bad feeling about that incident. If you think you're going to attract trash like that into my business and threaten my liquor license and livelihood, you're wrong. Because you'll be out that front door fast . . . kids or no kids."

"Dianne, I . . . I—"

"I told you not to lie to me!" She was almost yelling now, and for a second, I wondered if she was going to come around the desk and clip me. She didn't—clip me, that is. But she did get up and come around the desk. "Get out front and get the bar ready. And think about what I said. If you haven't told me by the end of your shift what it was all about, consider this your last day at the High Tide."

Desperation turned my blood to ice. "Dianne . . ."

I put my arms around her and pulled her close, rubbing suggestively against her.

"Are you crazy?" She put her hands on my chest and pushed me away hard.

Dianne waved at the door. "Get out, Dan. Now. And don't forget what I said."

She sat back at the desk and looked down at some papers in front of her, though I doubted she could be reading. I opened the office door, stumbled through the kitchen into the restaurant and around the partition to the bar.

Chapter 20

SHAMROCK SAT ON a stool at the L-shaped end of the bar. He had the *Boston Herald* spread out in front of him and a cigarette stuck between two nicotine-stained fingers. He looked up as I came in.

"Danny, my number was off by . . ." He stopped in mid-sentence. "What's the matter?"

I couldn't hide much from Shamrock either, not that I'd been planning on trying to hide anything from my best friend. If I couldn't talk to him, then who? A bottle of booze and a vial of cocaine would be the only alternative.

"Dianne," was all I said as I moved behind the bar.

"Ahh, Danny, what now?" Shamrock kept his voice low as if talking to a pitiful person. Maybe he was.

I glanced up at the Budweiser Clydesdale clock on the wall above the bar. "I'll tell you while I get the bar ready."

I talked as I filled sinks with ice, chopped fruit, restocked the beer chest, and did the handful of other chores I did every morning before I unlocked the door for business. Chores I could have done in my sleep.

After I'd told him what had transpired in Dianne's office and her ultimatum, he shrugged and nodded glumly. "The lass knows you like an Irishman knows his beer, my friend."

I didn't mention my little fling with Monica. "So what do I do?"

"What do you do?" Shamrock looked like I'd just asked him how much two and two was. "You're going to have to tell her the whole thing. Of course, you'll have to swear her to secrecy." He leaned across the bar a bit, lowered his voice. "About the . . . *gold*." He whispered the last word.

"Swear her to secrecy?" I looked at Shamrock like he was the dumb one. "Are you insane? Once she hears who Butchy Dunn is and what he's capable of, she'll have a conniption fit. Before she even hears about the . . . 'stuff'."

Shamrock blew a cloud of smoke. "I wouldn't be so sure, Danny. You know Dianne has bills like everyone else. And the slow season is starting. She might surprise you."

"True, she might," I said. "But I definitely wouldn't be surprised if she ended up working me over with one of the cast iron frying pans from the kitchen."

Shamrock shrugged. "You'll have to take that chance, Danny. Otherwise this is your last shift."

Shamrock was right. I knew Dianne meant what she said, so I had no choice. I'd have to hope her reaction to me attracting the likes of Butchy Dunn to her business wouldn't be murderous.

Someone banged on the front door.

"Eleven o'clock," Shamrock said. "Your fan club is here."

I turned to grab the front door key from the cash register, glancing toward the big picture window as I did. The cadaverous so-called lawman, if that was what he was, stood

just outside, staring in at me. He was dressed as before—
hat, buttoned up overcoat, cigarette butt hanging from his
mouth. Just staring.

I'll have the eyeball on ya.

I grabbed the key, hurried to the front door and unlocked
it, brushing outside before Eli could enter.

"Well, I never . . ." Eli began irritably.

Paulie stood behind Eli, just outside the door. I glanced
north up Ocean Boulevard and saw the old lawman hotfoot-
ing it in that direction.

"Paulie, do you know who that was?" I asked, gesturing
toward the departing figure.

"That odd duck?" Paulie answered. "Nope."

I waited.

"But I've seen him around," Paulie added. "A real whack
job. Seen him coming out of the Honeymoon Hotel a couple
times. Must be staying there."

A piece of good luck for a change. I felt a little better. I
had a bit more information, though what I could do with it
and where it might lead, I didn't have a clue.

Chapter 21

"GOLD?"

If I'd heard that word once, I'd heard it a dozen times in that same tone, this time from Dianne. We were seated in my so-called office—the rear red-vinyl booth on the bar side of the High Tide. My shift had just ended.

Shamrock sat next to Dianne, across from me. Coffee cups cooled in front of us. Shamrock had stayed to help me talk with Dianne and maybe keep my job. I hoped she'd be a bit more restrained with someone else present.

Dianne furrowed her brows. "Have you gone completely off your rocker?"

I looked helplessly in Shamrock's direction.

"It's true, Dianne." Shamrock hesitated, then added, "Well, the story's true. We're not sure if the gold is really there. But we think it is."

She kept her eyes on me. "You *think* it's there? Because some senile old man told you about Saint Gau . . . Gau . . ."

"Saint Gaudens twenty-dollar gold pieces," I offered hopefully.

"Whatever," she threw back at me. "And some trash from Charlestown, this Butchy Dunn, comes into my place, bangs you around and scares my customers because of some damn fairy tale? Do you really think I'm that stupid, Dan?"

I hated bringing Monica into our conversation again, but I had nothing to lose now. If I didn't convince Dianne there was some validity to the quest Shamrock and I were on, I was out the door in a few minutes, maybe for good. "I told you—the woman said her grandfather told her it was buried here. He was at the shootout with the cops and smugglers. That part's true. We saw the newspaper article about it over at the library. Cops and smugglers had a shootout back in 1930 over near my place somewhere."

Like I've said before, Dianne was equipped with a lie detector when it came to anything I said. She cocked her head. "And this Monica. You actually met her digging on the beach at night?"

I nodded. "Yes. Yes, I did."

"Where does she live?"

I hesitated. Was there any reason to lie? I couldn't think of one, and if I waited too long to answer, she'd sense there was more. "The Sea Urchin."

"Figures," she said disdainfully. "Have you been there?"

"With him." I pointed my thumb toward Shamrock.

"That's right," my friend said. "Danny and I went down together to see the lassie. She's Irish," he added, as if that should quell any doubts Dianne had.

"Oh, how wonderful." Dianne gave me a piercing look, then dropped it. I was glad I hadn't told Shamrock about my little tryst with Monica. He wasn't a good liar, either—especially where Dianne was concerned.

I didn't want to give Dianne too much time to think, so I spoke up. "That's why this Dunn guy was nosing around. He's sure the . . ." I lowered my voice, "*gold* is real, too. Why else would he be trying to scare me off?"

"Because he's obviously crazy, like you."

I glanced toward Shamrock, seeking help.

Shamrock turned toward Dianne, so animated he bumped—and almost spilled—his coffee. "Danny and I've been doing our homework. These gold coins are valuable num . . . numas . . . rare coins." He lowered his voice, glancing around like he was about to pass nuclear secrets to an enemy agent. "We figure they may be worth over a million dollars."

Shamrock stared at Dianne. I looked from one to the other. Dianne studied my face. No one spoke for what seemed an eternity. Shamrock, because he had nothing else to say. Me, afraid I'd put my foot in it and screw up the slight chance I had of keeping my job. And Dianne, I imagined, because she was debating my fate.

"A million dollars?" she finally said.

With those three words I knew I'd be back for my next shift.

"That's the number." Shamrock grinned. "At least. And Dan's been promised twenty-five percent of it."

"Of course I'm going to share it with you and Shamrock," I added, trying to sweeten the deal.

"What? Why?" Dianne asked.

"Because you're my friends and . . . and . . . Butchy Dunn came in here because of me and . . . and . . . and scared some of your customers, like you said."

She steepled her fingers against her chin, then dropped her hands to the table. "Maybe I'm crazy too, but I'll go along with this foolishness for a little bit. See if this is another one of your harebrained antics like I'm thinking it is. But if it isn't . . ."

The gold again. Even with a person straight as an arrow like Dianne that word is like a magnet. Especially with the possibility of a million-dollar value.

My shoulders sagged in relief, although it didn't last long.

"If I'm going to go along with this," Dianne continued. "I want to be involved too. Earn my share of the . . . you know what . . . if there is any." She hesitated. "And the first thing I want to look into is that measly twenty-five percent you mentioned. If we're going to find it, we deserve more . . . fifty percent at least."

"If we knew what 'piles' meant, we could find it for sure," Shamrock said. "That's the last piece of the puzzle."

We explained to Dianne how Monica's grandfather had mentioned the mysterious piles numerous times as a marker to the treasure's location. They weren't mysterious to Dianne, though. I'd forgotten she'd spent every summer as a child vacationing in the Island area with her family.

"Wait a second," she said. "That's what everyone called the wooden high tide breakers when we were kids—the piles. Back then they were so exposed all the kids used to run under them for their entire length. Now they're so buried you'd never know they were ever there."

"Jesus, you're right," I said, remembering the splinters I'd gotten through the years. A few inches of those rotten wood piles poked out from the sand. I'd forgotten that was what they were called back when I was a kid—the piles.

"Again, I want to earn my share," Dianne said. "I want to be involved. And I want to meet this Monica . . . talk to her about a bigger share for us." She couldn't have said it more disdainfully.

I was juggling nitroglycerin here. "Well . . . ah . . . I'm just helping out, Dianne. I wouldn't even know about the stuff except for her. And she does need it for her boy."

"That's what she says." Dianne gave me a skeptical look.

"I believe her," Shamrock said.

"You two fools would believe a mermaid."

"She wants to get her boy out of the city," I said. "Out of the projects. Into a better life."

"You can do that on less than seven hundred and fifty thousand dollars," Dianne said.

"I guess so, but—"

"It's not a guess." Dianne interrupted again. "What's she look like anyway, this Monica?"

The question seemed to come out of nowhere. I glanced at Shamrock. He was studying his cup of coffee.

"I don't know," I stammered. "Average looking, I guess."

"Like I said, if I'm going to be a part of this—at least for a while—I'll need to check this Monica out."

"Wait a minute, Dianne," I said, trying to keep any trace of desperation from my voice. "I promised her I wouldn't tell anyone except Shamrock."

"Well, you can just un-promise her. If there's any truth to this and we end up finding the treasure for her, we deserve way more than twenty-five percent. We deserve that much, Dan, just for keeping our mouths shut if nothing else. And don't forget the danger we face because of her brother. I want to talk to her."

I didn't know if Dianne was suspicious that I was hiding something from her or not, but I did know if she met

Monica, she wouldn't just be suspicious—she'd know. All I could hope to do was stall her.

"Let me talk to her first. Let her know that you're okay and that we had to tell you to save my job."

She eyed me doubtfully. "All right but hurry it up. I want to meet her. See if she's hoodwinked you two gullible idiots or if there really is anything to this."

"Sure, Dianne, sure," I said.

She started to get up, stopped, and looked from Shamrock to me and back again. "Anyone else know about this?"

"Danny was tellin' me some old coot waylaid him down on Ashworth," Shamrock said. "He was looking in the bar window this morning."

"Old coot?" Dianne sat down again. "Bar window? Who the hell is he?"

"Some old-timer who knew the grandfather in the nursing home and heard him ranting and raving." I didn't want to give Dianne any reason to regret the temporary reprieve she had just given me.

"Okay, I guess . . . maybe." She looked at me doubtfully. "Anyone else?"

I glanced at Shamrock. His lips were a white line. Waiting for my cue. But there was no sense in lying. She'd find out sooner or later, most likely sooner, considering who it was. I just hoped this wouldn't be a deal killer.

I cleared my throat. "Eddie Hoar and Derwood Doller."

"Eddie Hoar!" Dianne said, raising her voice. "Are you freaking—"

I tried to put out the fire I'd just started. "But they don't know much, Dianne. Next to nothing."

"Jesus Murphy . . . do they know about the . . .?"

"Well, yeah, but they think it's worth fifteen grand," I said, sounding desperate even to myself.

"Fifteen thousand is like a million to that Hoar bum," Dianne spat. "How the hell could you let him know about it, of all people?"

"Danny didn't tell him," Shamrock piped in. He quickly told her a sanitized version of Eddie Hoar's relationship with Butchy Dunn, leaving out the most violent parts. My friend was wise enough not to spook Dianne, especially after we'd apparently gotten her on board.

"Eddie Hoar," Dianne said, shaking her head. "The biggest loser on the beach. Just great." She quickly added, "He better not be getting any damn share."

"No, no," Shamrock and I both said in unison.

Dianne stood and stepped from the booth. "Remember, Dan, I'm going to do my fair share of work in this. If anything comes of it, I want to earn my share. I'm also going to keep an eye on you two buffoons, make sure you don't go off track like you've been known to do. And I'm not kidding, I want to talk to Monica ASAP."

"Sure, Dianne," I said, nodding like a bobblehead doll. "I'll arrange it."

Dianne scowled at me and headed toward the kitchen.

"That turned out okay, don't ya think, Danny?" Shamrock looked at me hopefully.

I shrugged. "About as good as it could, I guess. At least I still have my job."

"So it's all good then?" Shamrock said, beaming.

I didn't return his smile.

"What?" He knew me too well.

I couldn't hold the secret from my best friend any longer. I told him about my recent encounter with Monica.

When I was done, he looked at me pitifully. "You poor schmuck. You sure do have a knack for making things more complicated."

Chapter 22

ONE THING I had to find out. Not only did it worry me, I was curious. So I buried my gut instinct, the same instinct telling me to keep my big mouth shut and not risk letting anyone new find out about our treasure hunt.

I made arrangements to meet Steve Moore at the White Cap, a year-round restaurant and bar on a side street only a couple of blocks from the High Tide. Maybe I could kill two birds with one stone—get something done to protect Monica and Sam and also get info on who the hell the old coot was and how he fit into the picture.

I was sitting in a window booth that looked out on the street when Steve came in. It was about 5:15. He greeted me and sat cautiously in the chair across from me. It was cool for September and Steve wore a sport coat over a blue open-collar dress shirt. He was about my age with dark hair and a buzz haircut. Under that sport coat I was sure he had his police issue 9 mm in a holster.

Steve was a detective with the Hampton Police Department and we went way back. I had introduced him to his adopted son, Kelsey, back when I'd helped solve the murder of Kelsey's mother. Steve and his wife fell in love with the parentless boy and soon after adopted him. Ever since, Steve insisted that he and his wife owed me the world. I didn't look at it that way. Still, I had imposed on Steve more than once for help concerning nefarious goings-on in Hampton that I'd become involved in—innocently, of course. I hadn't liked asking for favors then and I didn't feel any better about it now.

Steve must have picked up on my vibe because he put his elbows on the table, folded his hands. "What kind of mess have you gotten yourself into this time?"

I forced a smile. "There's no trouble. I just wanted to touch base, say hi. It's been a while. I got a little sidetracked for a short bit, but I'm okay now. Can I ask for a small favor, though?"

"I knew it! What's that?"

"Order more than a Coke for a change. I'll pay for it."

"What the blazes are you talking about?"

"I don't want these waitresses to think we're cheapskates. I like coming here. Being a tip employee myself, I know how they talk about people who tie up a table and just order a drink."

Steve scowled. "Like me, you mean?"

"I hate to say it, Steve, but if the shoe fits . . ."

"Big deal. They're never busy anyway. There's always an empty table in here."

"Yeah, but it's just the idea. Doesn't matter if they need the table or not. I want to stay in good with them. I haven't got too many places on the beach that I like and feel comfortable in after some of the horror shows I pulled way back when. And I recently ran off the rails again."

"So I heard. You back with Dianne yet?"

"Not quite, but I'm working on it."

"You should work harder. She's a good woman and good for you."

"Does Kelsey know about my little slipup?" I asked.

"I don't think so. Even if he did, what you did for him outweighs one dumb mistake you made."

"I guess," I said glumly. "Embarrassing, though."

"I'm the one who should be embarrassed, now that you were kind enough to let me know that the waitresses here think I'm a cheapskate."

I smiled and Steve continued. "Come on. I know you didn't bring me down here just to see my face turn red."

I figured there was no easy way to put what I wanted to say, so I just said it. "I'm curious about a guy on the beach, Steve."

Steve smirked. "I'm curious about a lot of guys on the beach. You're one of them sometimes. So what?"

A waitress appeared and took our orders. She seemed quite pleased that Steve ordered a clam plate. Me not so much, seeing I'd offered to pay.

"This guy's a real odd duck," I started.

Steve took another sip of his drink, made a face. "How so?"

I hesitated. I wanted Steve's help and for that I had to give him some information. I didn't want him to learn about the gold, though. I had a tight wire to walk. "If you saw him, you'd know what I mean. He's old, in his eighties I imagine. Wears a dark topcoat buttoned up to his neck and an old beat-up fedora."

"You mean Fred?"

I was surprised. "You know him?"

"Of course I do. He stands out around here like an elephant strolling along Ocean Boulevard."

"Well, who is he?" I asked, trying to keep the anxiety from my voice. "Fred who?"

"Fred Capobianco."

"Wait . . . did you say Capobianco?"

"He's just an old-timer that's all. Used to be a state cop. Some of the older guys down at the station heard he used to get a piece of every booze load landed around here by one of the big syndicates back in Prohibition days."

"A cop," I said, trying to act nonchalant.

Now it all made sense, even the Capo reference. That's what Albert Keel meant—Capo wasn't a Mafia street boss. Keel was referring to this Fred Capobianco.

"Yeah. He's been hanging around the beach for a couple of weeks now. He's harmless."

So, the old coot was an ex-state cop and he'd been fired from the force. This likely meant he'd been crooked and gotten caught for the smuggling payoffs. That's how he would've known about the buried gold, especially if some of it had been intended as a pay-off he never got. This would explain why he considered the gold his. I wondered if I should pick Steve's brain further and decided not to pique his interest any more than I had to.

"Why?" he asked, looking at me with narrowed eyes.

"Just wondering," I lied. "Seen him around the beach and was curious."

"I hope you haven't bothered him."

The waitress came over with our dinner, gave me a smile and spared a smile for Steve, too.

"Jesus, of course not," I answered. "Just one more thing."

"I knew it. What?"

"Sorry," I said meekly. "Friend of Dianne's. Her brother has been bothering her."

"Who is he?"

I dreaded saying the name. "Butchy Dunn . . . or Billy Dunn. He goes by both names."

Steve's eyes opened wide. "What! So you haven't gotten yourself involved with anything, huh? Just a stone-cold killer from Charlestown. No way I can help you with him, Dan. I'd probably screw up ongoing investigations of half a dozen New England agencies . . . not to mention a few federal ones. All I can do is advise you to stay in your cottage until I let you know Dunn is back in prison for good. And watch your back."

He stood before I could protest. "Thanks for the dinner, but I have to go before this gets any worse." Steve headed for the door, then glanced back over his shoulder. "Watch your back, Dan. "You're playing in the dangerous big leagues now . . . and I do mean dangerous."

I watched him go out the door and across Ocean Boulevard to the parking area.

My gut churned. If Steve was that concerned about Dunn . . . if he really couldn't help me even if he wanted to . . . I was a sitting duck.

Chapter 23

THE DAY AFTER I met with Steve Moore, I decided to see if I could satisfy my curiosity about old man Capobianco, see what he was up to. I crossed Ocean Boulevard at the Tide, walked past the playground and around the back of the music stage seashell, and parked myself against the railing that ran along the beach between the sand and the boardwalk. I made sure I had a good view of the front of the Honeymoon Hotel. I hadn't brought Shamrock along because what I had in mind wasn't quite legal.

The weather was nice—blue sky and a moderate temperature. Fall is a beautiful time at Hampton Beach. It wouldn't last long though. Winter seemed to come earlier every year. Lasted longer, too. My age, again, I'm afraid. The snowy season wasn't as enjoyable as it once had been. Within the last year or two, I'd come to the conclusion that there was nothing as depressing as a summer resort in the winter. An unpleasant attitude for someone who called the beach his year-round home. Maybe even dangerous if said beach resident happened to be a gun owner and susceptible to depression on occasion, as I was.

I was trying to push those thoughts from my head when I spotted a figure coming out the front door of the Honeymoon Hotel.

Fred Capobianco, the mysterious old coot who had recently accosted me down on Ashworth, flashing a badge he probably got from a Cracker Jack box. He was dressed the same as last time I'd seen him. No one else would dress like that on Hampton Beach, summer over or not. He walked along Ocean Boulevard in the direction of the Casino. I followed on my side of the street. There weren't many pedestrians around, so I had to keep a safe distance. I didn't want him to make me.

When he reached the Casino complex, he walked up the few concrete stairs, went along the walkway to the far end of the building, and entered Funarama, a beach arcade. I hurried across the street, went up the stairs, and entered the arcade through one of the three wide doors.

Inside, I proceeded cautiously. The usual bells, whistles, and other assorted sounds of arcade machines assaulted my ears. A few teenagers were playing various games, but the number of customers was nothing compared to the hordes of coin-dropping kids playing the games on a summer day.

No old coot in sight.

I wove my way through the front of the arcade to a set of wooden stairs, maybe a dozen or so, that led to a lower-level room chock full of every conceivable arcade game you could think of. It wasn't hard to find the old man—there weren't many customers in this area either. He was in the middle of the lower room, already banging away at some old-style pinball machine.

I walked down the stairs, eased myself behind a wooden pillar in case he glanced my way, and watched, but not for long. He unbuttoned his topcoat, took it off, and placed it on the arcade machine beside him. He fished some coins from his pants pocket and placed them on the glass on the machine in front of him. He pumped in some of the coins.

That was all I had to see. It gave me the chance I was hoping for.

It took me less than five minutes to backtrack to the Honeymoon Hotel. The front door had a top-to-bottom crack in its glass. I opened the door and stepped inside. The place had seen its heyday long ago. The lobby had a few over-stuffed chairs scattered here and there. Each chair had its own floor lamp, several with tassels hanging from the lampshade. I'd seen similar lamps at my elderly aunt's place years ago.

A small wooden reception desk sat to my right. I went up to it. On the wall behind the desk was a wooden contraption with cubbyholes, each one sporting a number that most likely matched a room number. Almost all the keys were visible in the cubbyholes.

On top of the desk was a registration log. I glanced at it but didn't see the old man's name. Beside the log was a silver slap bell like the teachers used to have on their desks back in the day. I tapped it a few times.

Within a minute, a curtain hanging on a rod behind the desk slid open and a man stepped out, the man I had hoped would be working. He yawned and stretched as he came through the curtain and wandered up to the desk. He was thin, with a homely horse-like face and skin so pale you could win a lot of money betting he hadn't been on the beach one day this past summer.

He looked a little surprised when he saw me standing there. "Hey, Dan, what are you doing here? They foreclose on your place again?"

Artie was a real comedian and a regular at the High Tide. He'd drop in every afternoon before his shift at the Honeymoon and have a couple of Seagram's and water, no ice . . . ugh! Even being a bartender, I had no idea how anyone could enjoy a concoction like that, but Artie did. He looked like he'd been in the process of sleeping today's dose off when my slapping of the house bell roused him.

Usually, if I happened on a regular customer of mine somewhere in the real world, I'd banter a bit about nothing, just shoot the breeze. I didn't have time for that today. I had no idea how bad the old man's pinball addiction was or how long his quarters would hold out. I couldn't waste any time.

"The old guy who just left here, Artie, the one with the winter wardrobe?"

"Yeah, what about him?"

There was no one around I could see. I moved closer and rested my forearms on the reception desk. "I want to get into his room."

Artie's eyes widened and he lost any grogginess he still had.

"Just for a couple minutes," I added.

"Jeez, Dan. If you want to rip someone off, you picked the wrong character. This guy ain't got a pot to piss in. I gotta chase him every few days for his rent."

"I'm not going to take anything. You know me and you have my word. This guy's bothering a young lady I know, and I just want to find out a few things about him."

"Dianne?" Artie said, his voice going higher.

"No, not Dianne," I answered irritably. "I'll give you free drinks for a week. I just need a few minutes."

Artie cheered up. "A week?"

"Only two a day though," I said quickly. Then added, "And you can forget the tip."

I wasn't giving up much there. A week's worth of tips from Artie amounted to less than two dollars.

"All right," Artie said, his voice shaking. He fumbled with some keys on a keychain attached to his belt, removed one and handed it to me. I assumed it was a pass key. "Room number nine . . . top of the stairs . . . way down back. Bring back the key and hurry up. I'll ring if anyone comes. And please don't take nothing, Dan. I got my job to think about."

I took the key, hot footed up a short, steep flight of stairs, and hurried toward the end of the hall, barely noticing the numbers on the other rooms as I passed. At the end of the hall was a door marked, Fire Exit. The room to the left was marked eight. Turning to the room on my right, I was flummoxed for a second.

Number six.

I looked back at the rooms I'd passed, then took a look again at the door on my right. I went up to the door and fingered the metal number six attached there. Sure enough, it was loose. I slid it up to its correct position—nine. I let the number fall again and quickly used the key Artie had given me.

I found myself in a lower-end winter rental room, complete with an unmade bed with a mattress that almost touched the floor. There was one chair like the ones down in the lobby and another ancient floor lamp with a tasseled shade. A small fridge and a hot plate sat near a sink with old-style fixtures. In the middle of the room was a card table.

The first thing that caught my eye on the table was a half-eaten can of dog food with a fork stuck in it—that explained Capobianco's breath. Beside that was an old-style rotary phone; the house room phone I assumed. More interesting, though, was a spiral notebook with section tabs. I noticed one marked Marlowe. A quick examination made it obvious that this old fart was keeping me under tight surveillance. There were notations of the times I came and left my cottage and work. I realized with a chill that had nothing to do with the weather that he must have listened at my windows. There were notes about my phone conversations, some of which concerned my kids and other matters this snoop had no right to hear.

I thumbed through the notebook. One tab read, Nichols Dame. The note was dated yesterday and written in wobbly handwriting.

Talked to her son for approx 15 min.

Apparently he was not only peeking in Monica's window, but sticking his ears in, too. I'd have to tell Monica to close her window and shades tight.

Another tab marked The Mick was a detailed surveillance report on Shamrock's comings and goings. My friend must have kept his windows closed because there was no mention of any phone conversations, although a shade must have been up because he noted a Potato Peeler Flag on the wall. That had to refer to the large Irish tri-color Shamrock proudly displayed above his fireplace.

I was about to take a peek at the rest of the notebook when the telephone rang. Artie?

Maybe, maybe not. I couldn't take a chance. I set the notebook down on the card table and got out of there, locking the room door as I did. I was going to leave the way I came in, but I heard heavy footsteps coming up the stairs and got a glimpse of a fedora rising up the stairs. I hightailed it out the Fire Exit and down a short fire escape.

On the way back to my cottage, I tried to figure out what I'd stumbled upon. I wasn't sure—was Fred Capobianco working for someone? Maybe Butchy Dunn? Or was he just a lone wolf poking around, trying to get money he believed was his? And if he knew about the gold, how much did he know? Did he realize its actual value?

Maybe, maybe not, I decided. He wasn't playing with a full deck, after all. I was more puzzled now, at least about the old man, than I had been before I'd cased his room.

The only thing I knew for sure was that I'd have to remember to give Artie his key back when he came in for the first of his free drinks. And to reimburse Dianne for those drinks. What else was new?

I also needed to tell the friends involved in this treasure hunt to watch out for Capobianco and close their windows and shades. For now, we would have to meet and talk out of the range of prying eyes and ears.

Chapter 24

I WENT TO my cottage for a few minutes before deciding it was time to visit Monica again. I walked down to Ashworth Ave.

When Monica answered the door, she motioned me in. I saw her eye right away. A black eye to beat all black eyes. Her right eye was more purple than black and almost swollen shut. The little I could see of the eye itself was red and mucus laden.

"Jesus, what happened?" I asked.

"If I told you I walked into a door, would you believe me?"

I reached over, put my hand gently on her chin, and tried to raise her head to get a better view of the damage.

She shoved my hand away.

"Have you had that looked at?"

She shook her head. "It's all right. I've had black eyes before."

"Not like that, I hope."

"Never mind that, Dan. He . . . he . . ." she started to sob.

I'm pretty dumb in situations like this but instinctively, I guess, I took her into my arms and pulled her close in what

I thought was almost a brotherly embrace. Apparently, she thought differently. Her lips came up to mine and we kissed softly, both afraid to hurt that bruised eye. With an eye like that, I knew this wasn't going anywhere. I had more on my mind anyway, especially after seeing that peeper.

"Your brother do this to you?"

She pushed me away. "I wouldn't tell him what he wanted to know. I kept telling him I didn't know anything. Next thing I know, he slugged me. But worse—he threatened Sam."

"His own nephew?" Guess someone had to hit me over the head to convince me a human being could be that much of a lowlife.

"Oh, Dan. Don't be so . . . so . . ." She burst into sobs again.

This time I could feel them as I held her. I led her over to the couch, sat her down, went to the tiny kitchen area, got her a glass of water, and sat beside her. She took a couple of small sips and pushed the glass back in my hands. I put it on the scarred coffee table.

I put my arm around her shoulder and did my clumsy best to console her. After a few minutes, she calmed down and I removed my arm.

"You've got to go to the cops, Monica. There's no other way. If he did this to you, he could come back and do worse. And Sam . . ." I regretted saying that the instant I said it.

Monica startled and her good eye widened. She grabbed my arm. I could feel her nails digging into me. "I can't do that, can't go to the cops. We've got to find that gold before Billy or someone else does. I have to get Sam out of those projects. He'll end up like Billy or worse. They've got the same blood. Sammy could go either way. I can't let him end up like that. Please."

"What about now? What about keeping him safe now?" I asked. I was thinking of my own son, Davey, and how I'd feel and what I'd do if someone threatened him.

"He's with my sister-in-law. I told you about her. Billy would never bother him there."

"Don't even tell me where she lives." I consider myself a stand-up guy, but let's face it—who really knows what they'll do with the business end of a cocked revolver in their mouth? "Don't tell me. The fewer people who know where Sam is, the better."

"You won't go to the police about this?" Monica asked.

"Listen," I began. "I have a cop friend, and we can trust him. He could help. Maybe put some heat on your brother to make him think twice about hanging around here or doing anything to you or Sam. Especially when I tell him about that." I pointed at her unsightly eye. I wondered if Steve would reconsider getting involved if he knew what Dunn had done to his own sister.

After a few minutes of silence, Monica said, "Your friend only. If you're sure you can trust him. Promise . . . no other cops. Billy was very threatening about that."

"Fine. I promise."

What else could I do? I knew what Dunn was capable of, although I hadn't realized that he'd actually harm his own sister and possibly his nephew to get his hands on the gold—if there was any gold. But Monica's shiner proved what he was really capable of.

This confirmed an idea I'd had earlier—Dunn may very well know the true value of the gold. No one, not even a scumbag like Dunn would slug his sister like that or threaten his young nephew over twenty grand. Or was I just being naive again?

"All right," I said. "But I've got a gun I want you to keep for a while."

She shook her head adamantly. "Absolutely not. I hate guns. Growing up where I did, I've seen what they can do. I won't touch one."

I sighed, then nodded. Lots of people felt that way. I wasn't one of them.

This situation was getting very heavy, very fast. Anything could happen.

"Have you found out anything?" Monica asked. It was a legitimate question, but I got the feeling she was trying to change the subject. I couldn't blame her.

I smiled. "I think I've found out where the Seaview cottage was."

Monica tried to smile, too, but with her eye it looked like a grotesque grimace. "Can we start digging then?"

Unfortunately, I wasn't sure I could fully trust her. Didn't know if she could stand up to her brother's questioning if he got hold of her again, either. I decided to play it close to the vest, not give her all the pieces of the puzzle . . . in case she told Dunn for one reason or another.

"Where is it, Dan?"

I didn't answer right away and she studied my face for a long moment. "Don't you freaking trust me?"

"Of course I do, but even if I'm right about where the Seaview was and your grandfather gave us the right distance down from the cottage, there's a long beach down there and we'd probably need excavating equipment to dig up the length of the Seaview. Not to mention, it would tip off the entire beach. Unless . . . we can narrow it down a little." I kept Dianne's revelation about the 'piles' to myself but wondered if Monica could narrow the location down even further.

"How?"

"Didn't your grandfather tell you anything else?"

"No. Nothing . . . nothing." She shook her head and winced. "You asked me that before." She looked like she might start sobbing again.

"He must have told you something. Keep thinking."

She shook her head, winced again. "Dan, I can't . . . I can't think of anything. Maybe we could go down there and look."

"Shamrock and I have already walked up and down that area of the beach so much we've worn a deep trench in it and found nothing."

We stood in awkward silence for a long moment.

"I've got to get going," I finally said.

She grabbed my hand. "Do you want to stay?" She forced a semblance of a smile, trying, I thought, to look sincere.

"Afraid Butchy will be back?" I asked.

If she'd answered yes, I would have stayed and it wouldn't have been for a selfish reason either. With that super tender eye, I knew we wouldn't get all hot and steamy.

I guess she knew it too because she said, "No, he definitely won't be back today. I know how he thinks. You can go. Don't worry."

I turned and headed for the door. Then paused. "Do you know an old guy wears a fedora and topcoat? Looks like something out of a 1940 detective movie? Might have been a cop at one time?"

"No," she answered. "What's a fedora, anyway? And what's he got to do with this?"

"He's following us—me, you, Shamrock."

"Following us? Me?"

"He's a freelancer who found out about the gold and wants to cut himself in for a piece. He might be working with Butchy, though. Keep your eyes open and don't lead him anywhere, especially to Sam."

Her smooth forehead lined and she shuddered. "Jesus Christ."

"Okay, gotta get going," I said. "Keep your door locked. Call if you need me. And draw your shade all the way and lock your window."

She looked at me quizzically. "What the heck kind of creep is this old guy, anyway?"

"Just that, an old creep. I hope. Harmless . . . I think. But just do what I asked, please."

"I will," she said.

I gave her a peck on the cheek before leaving and locked the button lock on the door. "Use the deadbolt."

Walking along the sidewalks of Hampton Beach in the direction of home, I wondered if we were ever going to find this so-called treasure. And if we did, would it be before someone else was hurt as badly as Monica had been? Or God forbid, even killed. With Butchy Dunn in the mix, that was a distinct possibility.

Time was of the essence if I wanted all of my friends—and myself—to avoid any unpleasant outcomes.

I had to either find this treasure or learn that it was just a fool's tale. The longer I took to uncover the truth about this treasure, the more chance one, or more, of my friends could be hurt badly or worse. I couldn't allow that to happen. I wouldn't.

The cold wind coming off the ocean the rest of the way home matched the chill in my soul.

Chapter 25

I STALLED DIANNE as long as I could, but finally she gave me an ultimatum—introduce her to Monica or else.

We were at the Sea Urchin, Shamrock along for support. He and I sat on the sofa in Monica's studio. Across from us, side-by-side on the twin chairs, were Dianne and Monica.

Sam, who'd just come back from his aunt's, was sitting on a vinyl-covered chair at the Formica kitchen table. I'd been pleased to find him here when we'd arrived. I was certain his presence would help diffuse Dianne's anger if she did pick up on anything between Monica and me; so far I'd been right. Sam resembled his mother, even though his medium-length hair and eyes were brown. His skin was darker than his mother's, too. But he'd certainly gotten her good looks. He had a winning personality and seemed comfortable around adults.

Of course, Monica looked great even with the black eye— something her brother seemed to be an artist in creating. But even that couldn't disguise the fact that she was a very attractive woman.

Monica looked more uncomfortable than Dianne. I imagined Dianne was trying to pick up on any vibes between

Monica and me and did everything I could to look nonchalant. But women? I couldn't understand them. The two actually seemed to be getting along well. Was Sam having the calming effect I'd hoped he would? Dianne had the potential to be very explosive in a situation like this. It had happened before. Of course, she'd always said I had instigated the outcome. She'd probably always been right.

"How do you like the beach, Sam?" Dianne asked.

"I like it, Ms. Dennison," Sam said, "except not all the arcades are open."

"Please call me Dianne. I feel old enough as it is." Dianne gave me a quick glance.

"Arcades are kind of slow in the off-season," I said, pretending to ignore her look. "But you'd love it in summer."

"Maybe we'll come up for a while in the summer, honey," Monica said to Sam.

"If you do," Dianne said. "You'll have to come to the High Tide for a nice meal. Do you like lobster or fried clams?"

"Both!" Sam answered.

"Okay," Dianne said. "I'll make lobster rolls and fried clam plates for you and your . . . mom."

Will wonders never cease. I didn't miss Dianne's emphasis on the word, mom. Obviously, she liked the boy as much as I did. How she felt about Monica, I couldn't be sure. But again, because of Sam's presence, the likelihood of Dianne exploding because of Monica was much less probable than I had previously feared.

For some spur-of-the-moment reason, maybe because I felt she deserved to know, I told Monica about the possible value of the gold. I spoke softly—little pitchers with big ears and all—but Monica still got the message. Even though

Dianne already knew everything I was saying, she looked genuinely thrilled and shocked.

Monica's hand went to her forehead. She glanced at Sam seated at the kitchen table. "Oh . . . my . . . god . . . no." Her voice shook and she looked about to cry. "Sam, please go outside for a few minutes."

The boy did as he was told.

"What's wrong?" I asked. "I thought you'd be happy."

"Billy will have his entire army of street thugs up here looking for it now. And I do mean he has an army. They'll dig up the entire beach if they have to. And hurt anyone they feel is in the way."

"Saints preserve us," Shamrock said. "But maybe he doesn't know the true value yet?"

I knew Shamrock was saying this for the ladies' benefit. We'd already agreed that Dunn had probably been the earlier visitor to the coin shop asking about twenty-dollar gold pieces. If we were correct, then he knew the treasure's true value. Neither of us wanted to get Monica or Dianne more worried than they already were, though.

Monica, of course, knew her brother better than we did. "Believe me," she said. "If we know, then Billy knows. Like I said before, he's street smart. Doesn't miss a trick. We have to move fast; find it before Billy goes full-out. Otherwise, that could be the end of all of us."

"I have a business to run," Dianne said.

"And Danny and I have to work," Shamrock added.

"You don't know my brother like I do," Monica said, sounding desperate. "Not only will he keep all the gold, he won't want any of us around to tell the cops he has it . . . believe me."

Dianne gasped and my heart sped up. Shamrock muttered, "I believe you."

"If you stick with me," Monica continued, "and keep looking, we'll split anything we find four ways."

"You don't have to—" I started, then noticed the wide-eyed looks on both Dianne and Shamrock's faces, telling me to shut up.

It took only another minute to agree to a four-way split on any gold we recovered. I just hoped we'd all be alive to enjoy it. Monica had certainly added fuel to the fire, building up Butchy Dunn's notorious reputation. I quickly realized that Monica's offer wasn't as generous as I'd first thought—we'd probably earn every penny, if there even was any gold to find.

"I have to get going," Dianne said. "Can I talk to you outside for a minute, Dan?"

"Sam, can you come back inside, please," Monica called. Sam came in and climbed into his seat at the table.

"Bye, Sam," Dianne said. "Don't forget you and your mom are coming in for lobster rolls and clams. We have the best on the beach."

"I won't forget," Sam answered. "Thank you very much."

Monica gave her son a look of pride. I couldn't blame her. He was a keeper. The final look Dianne gave the boy told me she agreed.

"Nice to meet you, Monica," Dianne said.

"Same here," Monica replied.

I had a brilliant inspiration, something that would delay whatever Dianne wanted to 'talk' about. "How about if I take you ladies over to Wally's for dinner and drinks? Shamrock can watch Sam—if that's okay with you, Monica."

Dianne hesitated a moment, then nodded. "I could let them know at work . . ."

"Fine with me," Monica agreed.

They both glanced at Sam.

"How about if we bring pizza back for supper?" I asked.

Sam beamed. "That'd be super. I love Wally's pizza."

"And don't forget me with that pizza, too." Shamrock said.

"What say, ladies?" I asked. "Shall we go?"

The three of us went down the motel stairs and headed to Ashworth Ave. Wally's was across the street and maybe a block or two south.

As if I couldn't be more surprised than I already was—things were going way too smoothly—I felt each of the women take one of my hands to cross the street. Monica had my right hand and led our little parade as we stepped onto Ashworth Ave.

Something black flashed to my right. Monica was torn from my hand, thrown so hard by a speeding car that my shoulder felt like it dislocated. She sailed through the air, landing with a sickening thud in the middle of the road fifty feet from where she'd started.

Dianne screamed as she ran to Monica's side and knelt. She reminded me of that iconic photo of the woman looking up from the student who was shot at Kent State in 1970. Dianne's face was just as stunned. There were shouts from patrons at Wally's and many ran out to help.

But when I reached Monica's side, I knew it was too late.

Sirens shrieked, ambulance and police arrived. Everyone was questioned by the police about the hit-and-run, with no one able to provide information on the driver, only the black color of the car.

The rest of the night was horrible, to say the least. Thank god, Dianne was there to console Sam. I certainly couldn't have done it.

I was a basket case. Not only was I feeling guilty that I should have done something to prevent Monica's getting hit, but I was also overwhelmed by the feelings that welled up inside, feelings I didn't realize I'd had. But I didn't have time to deal with feelings.

Shamrock and I made sure Dianne and Sam got to her condo safely. She'd agreed to keep him with her until Monica's sister-in-law came to pick him up. We stayed with them until they both fell asleep—we did too, me in a chair, Shamrock on the couch.

At my urging, Steve Moore had convinced the police chief to assign a cruiser to watch the front of the building until they figured out if there was any further danger. By the time the sun came up, Steve, who'd joined us in the condo, Shamrock, and even myself, had come to the conclusion that I was probably the intended target of the murderous driver. We were convinced it had been Butchy Dunn or one of his stooges behind the wheel in the hit-and-run that had taken Monica's life. Butchy, knowing I was an expert on Hampton Beach, most likely feared that I would lead Monica to the treasure.

Chapter 26

THE NEXT DAY I was behind the bar at the Tide doing my morning setup. I'd had a sleepless night thinking about Monica's horrible death. I felt so guilty about taking her away from her place—and from Sam. We could have called out for pizza or I could have picked it up and brought it back. The place was practically across the street . . .

Paulie and Eli were my only customers and neither had hinted about the big secret—aka gold on Hampton Beach. That was good. If anyone heard rumors on Hampton Beach before Eli and Paulie heard them, I'd never met that person. If my early customers didn't know anything, it was unlikely anyone else on the beach was wise yet.

They had heard about Monica's hit-and-run, though. Fortunately, they didn't tie the accident to me and I didn't enlighten them.

Eli was giving his usual lecture on game show strategy with the TV show we watched every morning at this time when the big wooden front door opened, letting in two of Hampton's finest. I knew them both, though not by name. One of the officers was young and had a tattoo peeking out from the wrist of his long-sleeved uniform shirt. I assumed he pumped iron; the shirt material stretched tight across his large chest. The other cop, older with wispy white hair, didn't see the gym much. His shirt was stretched, too—in the stomach area. They knew where they were headed and marched right up to the bar.

"Dan Marlowe?" the older cop asked, even though I was pretty certain he knew who I was.

"That would be me," I answered warily.

"The lieutenant wants to see you down at the station . . . pronto."

Eli turned and was eyeing the two cops up and down. The younger one gave Eli a hard look and Eli looked away. Still, I knew the old beer drinker wasn't going to miss a word of what was said.

"What about?" I asked.

"The lieutenant will tell you that when you get there."

"I'm working. I can't leave now."

"You're going to have to," the old cop said. "The lieutenant said he'd be up here to see you if you didn't."

I wasn't sure if that was a bluff or not, but I didn't want to find out. I knew it wouldn't be about Monica's tragedy; he could have gotten all that info from Steve. Common sense told me it might have something to do with the treasure search. If that was the case, the last thing I'd want is Lieutenant Richard Gant, my old nemesis, coming to the Tide. He'd had a burr in his hide concerning me for years. Any crime on the beach—from handbag thefts on the sand in summer to vacant cottage breaks in the winter—Gant blamed on me. He definitely thought I was behind anything criminal of significance that happened on the beach, all dating back to my earlier addiction and a couple of poor choices I'd made. As far as Gant was concerned, once a criminal, always a criminal.

I didn't want Gant coming and blabbing so everyone could hear whatever it was he was blaming me for this time.

"All right," I said. "But I have to tell the boss. Someone's got to take over while I'm gone."

I took off my apron and headed around the bar.

The old cop held up a hand. "You can stay here." He nodded at the muscle-bound cop. "You get him."

"It's a her," I said. "And she's in the office—you have to go through the kitchen."

The young cop headed off in the direction of the kitchen.

"Hey, Dan. Would you mind givin' me another before you go?" Eli wiggled his glass.

For a moment I thought he was kidding, but one look at his face told me otherwise. "You've barely taken a sip out of the one in front of you."

"I know, I know." Eli nodded. "But you don't put no head on the beer. Everyone else does. I don't wanna pay for foam after you're gone."

I sighed, moved back to the spigots, and poured Eli his headless beer. I glanced at Paulie who shook his head. A bottle drinker, he didn't have any foam issues.

The old cop stood there, staring at the TV above the bar.

Finally, Eli leaned across the bar and crooked his index finger, beckoning me closer. I leaned in, not wanting the cop to hear whatever the hell it was Eli was about to say.

"What's this all about, Dan?" he whispered. "What did you do now?"

"Nothing," I growled. I was thinking about questioning the older cop again but decided against it. With my luck he'd say something I wouldn't want to fall on Eli and Paulie's ears. So, I kept my mouth shut.

A minute later, Dianne stormed around the partition that separated the dining room from the bar area. Right behind her was the young cop and behind him, Shamrock.

"What's this all about?" Dianne demanded. She glared at the older cop, looking as good as ever with her hair tied back with a blue ribbon, tomato sauce-stained white restaurant shirt, and blue jeans.

"The lieutenant wants to speak with your bartender down at the station," the old cop said. He ran his hand through his thin hair.

"About what?" Dianne planted her fists on her hips.

The old cop shrugged. "I don't know, miss. We were just told to get your bartender here and bring him in. Just gonna ask some questions, I think."

"You have no right to do that," Dianne said, with a firm shake of her head. "He doesn't have to go with you. I'm trying to run a business here. I need my bartender."

The old cop seemed flummoxed. I had to help him, Dianne, and myself out. "It's no good, Dianne," I said. "If I don't go down . . . they said he'll come up here."

"So let him," Dianne said, nodding her head.

"I don't know what it's all about," I said, "but we don't want to disturb the customers." I raised my eyebrows. Would Dianne realize the questioning might have something to do with our gold quest? If it did, we certainly didn't want the Tide's customers listening in.

4

Whether she realized that possibility or thought I might have gotten involved in something else unsavory, she changed her tune. "How long will he be down there?"

"I don't know, miss," the old cop said. "Only as long as the lieutenant needs him."

"You'll be okay, Dan?" Dianne asked in a calmer voice.

"Sure," I answered. "I'm used to this by now." I'd taken more than one trip to the Hampton police station in the past.

"One more quick one, Dan?" Eli asked as I again headed around the bar. I ignored him and looked at Shamrock. He had a worried look on his face. I gave him a grin; he forced one in return.

I strode toward the front door, the two cops trailing behind me.

"I'll get back as soon as I can." I gave Dianne what I hoped was a reassuring smile.

"Don't worry," she answered. "We'll be fine."

Just as I reached the door, I thought of one more thing. Just in case this turned out to be more than an unimportant questioning. "Call James Connolly," I called out.

Chapter 27

IT WAS A short ride from the High Tide to the Hampton Police Station, down a side street to the one-story cinder-block building on Ashworth Avenue. I was let out of the back seat of the cruiser and ushered in the front door and down a corridor. We stopped in front of a glass door stenciled with two words that made my stomach flip—*Lieutenant Gant.*

The older cop knocked on the glass. A voice I recognized growled, "Come in."

The cop opened the door, stepped aside, and I moved past him into the room. The door closed behind me with a loud *snick!*

Gant sat behind a metal desk. The room smelled of stale cigarette smoke, body odor, and ripe sneakers. The desktop was cluttered with a black telephone, gooseneck lamp, and a jumble of papers. A picture of a cop with scrambled eggs on his cap hung on the wall behind Gant; the chief I assumed.

Beside the chief hung a photo of President Clinton. I wasn't a fan of either.

"Sit down," he said reluctantly as if he hated to make the offer.

I took a seat in one of the two rolling chairs facing the desk. I wished I could use the chair to roll right out of the room. On the other hand, I was curious as to what this was all about. It couldn't be too big a deal. I'd been in this building before on what you could call serious suspicion and had been questioned in an interrogation room. The office seemed less formal and intimidating. I hoped I was right.

Gant sat with his forearms on the desk, glaring at me through narrowed eyes. His gun-metal gray hair was slicked straight back. He wore a light blue dress shirt with a red tie. A navy-blue blazer hung from the back of his chair.

"You've put your foot in it again, Marlowe," he growled. "Big time now."

He stared hard at me, likely waiting for me to respond. I wasn't going to say a word until I had a better idea of what he thought I had stepped in.

We stared at each other long enough that he must have decided I was playing the dummy act.

"Where were you yesterday afternoon?"

I didn't answer right away. I could tell by the reddening of his face he didn't like my hesitation.

"Where were you yesterday, Marlowe?" Gant bellowed.

If I delayed any longer he'd burst a blood vessel. "I was working or home."

"Can anyone verify that? Before I could respond he added, "And not that damn Irish dishwasher sidekick of yours or your girlfriend, either."

"At work, yes. At home, I was alone." I was beginning to suspect what this was about—someone had reported my breaking into Fred Capobianco's room.

"That's convenient," Gant said. "But you couldn't have had anyone verify your whereabouts unless they were gonna verify you were at the Honeymoon Hotel. In a room you should not have been in." His voice rose. "Where you beat a helpless old man to death!"

I almost shouted, then decided it might be better not to respond. Artie had most likely ratted me out. At least I wouldn't have to give him free drinks now.

But beating an old man? To death? Had Gant gone completely over the edge?

Gant pulled a paper from the stack on his desk, looked at it. "Frederick Capobianco. Ring a bell, smart guy?"

I must have made some kind of smirk Gant didn't like. He leaned forward so close I could have punched him if I was so inclined. But I didn't. Obviously.

"Answer the question, you piece of shit." Gant sputtered as he spoke and flecks of spit went flying. I leaned back. "What were you doing in this guy's room?"

"I don't know what you're talking about, Gant. Have you gone simple?"

"You won't think it's so funny, big shot, when the state lab guys check your blood type. You left some blood and skin on that poor old man's teeth."

My anxiety was rising. Capobianco was dead. Beaten to death and I knew who most likely did it—Butchy Dunn. That was his style. But Gant was going to try and pin it on me—Murder One. My body started to shake.

"Look, Gant, you're crazy if you think . . ."

"Lieutenant Gant to you, Marlowe," he bellowed again. "I want to know what you were doing in this man's room."

"I wasn't in it."

"I got you dead to rights this time, punk," Gant roared. "An eyewitness saw you go in the room."

I apparently hadn't offered Artie enough free drinks.

"What's that?" Gant reached over, grabbed my right hand, and looked at my skinned knuckles.

"I got those moving a beer keg," I answered. "Look, Ga . . . Lieutenant. It wasn't me." I had no desire to antagonize him on his turf, so I played nice. "Your so-called witness must have been mistaken."

"Mistaken? Bullshit! He made a hundred percent ID on you. You even bribed him for the key to the room. If he wasn't an ex-con with a perjury conviction on his sheet, you'd already be under arrest. This time you picked the wrong place for a score. The guy used to be a state cop. The staties won't give up on this 'til you fry. You're off to the can this time, Marlowe. For life . . . if you're lucky." Gant pursed his lips and leaned back in his chair, his fingers gripping the desktop.

Anger slowly replaced the anxiety. I wasn't going to get railroaded by Gant.

"Ex-cop?" I said hotly. "Fifty years ago maybe . . . and tossed out for being a crook. He probably had a thousand enemies."

Gant's eyebrows shot up. I was on a roll and out of control.

"The old man was eating dog food and tailing people around the beach," I spit out before I realized I shouldn't have.

Gant jumped up, came around the desk, and lowered his face to mine. I'm ashamed to say I winced, although his cigarette and coffee breath could've accounted for that. "How the hell do you know he was following people and ate . . . ate . . ."

"Dog food," I finished for him.

"How do you know this?" Gant was so close I could've counted the busted blood vessels on his nose to pass the time.

"Just talk around the beach," I said, attempting to backpedal.

"You were in his room," Gant yelled. "Admit it. You're not only a murderer, Marlowe, you're a stupid murderer. Why did you kill him?"

Just then the door behind me opened and I heard a familiar voice say, "Don't answer that!"

Gant bolted upright. "Didn't your mother teach you to knock before you come in, Connolly?" His voice had gone ice cold which made me even more nervous.

James Connolly, Esquire, came up and stood beside my chair. His black, bushy hair was wild as usual, and his battered brown briefcase was in his hand. His sport coat could have used pressing. "Not when I hear my client being browbeaten."

"Eavesdropping again, huh, Connolly? That's typical of you." Gant stepped back around the desk and retook his seat.

"You got any charges against my client, Lieutenant?"

"Not yet," Gant almost snarled, "but I will. And it's a biggie this time, Counselor. Murder One."

"Whatever it is, you'll have to prove it, Lieutenant. By the book."

Gant gave us a disdainful look, then swatted the air dismissively. "Get out of here . . . both of you. Now!"

"Gladly," my attorney said. "Come on, Dan."

I got up, avoiding Gant's piercing gaze, and quietly followed James out of the office and out of the police station. He led me to his car. It was the same heap he'd had the last time I needed his services. We both hopped in.

"Gant thinks I broke into some hotel room on the beach and beat an ex-state cop to death."

"Great," he said, glancing at his watch. "You got yourself involved in murder this time, buddy. You're moving up in the world. Did you do it?"

"Do you really think I could beat someone to death?"

James shook his head. "No, but if you're playing amateur detective again, anything could happen."

"I was just trying to help a friend."

"Well, you better try and unhelp him. You might get picked up again before the day's out . . . if Gant thinks he's got enough on you."

"He doesn't," I said with more confidence than I felt. "The person who says he saw me wouldn't look believable in a witness box."

"You'd be surprised. I've seen Hell's Angels come into court looking and talking like they had theology degrees from Harvard."

"Maybe. But the blood at the scene wasn't mine and the results will confirm it."

"Now you're a lab technician? I hope you're right."

"Let's talk outside for a minute," I said. The air inside the car was stale and smelled of old farts. We hopped out to get some fresh air.

James sniffed heavily, glanced at his watch again. "Look, I have to be in Lawrence. You want to take a ride and have a quick sniff?"

James was one of those rare people who could do cocaine without going overboard. For now. So he functioned and he was a good lawyer. At least he'd always treated me well. We'd become friends during the course of a couple of tight spots I'd found myself in on the beach. And he worked cheap and came when I needed him.

Still, every time we were together, I found myself studying him to see if there was any deterioration evident from his drug indulgence. I'd never seen too much of a change. He was eccentric from the first time I met him, I guess you could say. I knew from experience some people could hide a severe cocaine problem successfully for quite a while. Until they started parading down Ocean Boulevard in broad daylight in their birthday suit. I'd reached that level, though fortunately, birthday suits didn't have anything to do with my downfall. My decline was worse. Someone who has gone through an addiction always thinks what they went through was worse than what anyone else went through. Anyway, I kept my fingers crossed for James. He was a good man.

For a moment, I thought of saying yes to his offer of a hit. Apparently, my stomach did too . . . it growled and my bowels rolled. I caught myself, "No. Thanks."

"All right," James said as he opened his squeaky car door. He hopped back in and started the engine, which sounded awfully loud for a small car. James leaned out the window. "I'll send you a bill."

I waved and he roared off with a squeal of tires.

On the walk back to the Tide, I thought about the Hampton police lieutenant who hated me, the dead ex-state cop I was accused of murdering, the Charlestown gangster who was as violent as Whitey Bulger, my wonderful used-to-be girlfriend, two beach clowns hiding out in a Seabrook mobile home, and a beautiful woman also dead.

All that and buried treasure. So much gold, if it were there, it'd take a few very strong men to lift it, and likely as hard to hold onto as a rabid hyena—if we got hold of it.

Chapter 28

BY THE TIME I got back to the High Tide, I'd been gone longer than I thought. I bumped into Eli and Paulie coming out the front door.

"You guys leaving early?" I asked, trying to avoid the obvious topic.

"She's got Ruthie on the bar," Eli said scornfully. "Another foam head. Half the damn beer is white nothin'. I ain't gonna put up with that."

He looked me up and down. "Let's go back in now that Dan's here," he said to Paulie.

I didn't look forward to Eli drilling me silly about my trip to police headquarters.

"Nope, I've had enough," Paulie answered, putting a grin on my face. "If you want a ride home, I'm going now. I have a dentist appointment."

"All right, all right," Eli said irritably. "Hold your damn horses."

He turned to me. "What the hell happened down the hoosegow? You in trouble again, Dan?" His eyes sparkled with anticipation, as best bloodshot eyes can.

I waved my hand and started through the front door. "No time now, Eli. I'll tell you next time I see you."

"Wait a . . ." was all I heard as the heavy front door closed behind me.

Inside, lunch was just winding down. Patrons were leaving the dining room and Ruthie was wrapping up a dozen or so customers that were finishing their meals and drinks at the bar. She hustled back and forth along the back side of the bar, her red hair flying.

"You might as well finish these customers, Ruthie," I said, not wanting to interrupt her work.

She gave me a smile and nodded. Ruthie had given up one or two of her dining room tables to fill in for me so, of course, she was entitled to the bar customers' tips. Some of my good tippers were still on stools, so I was confident she'd do well.

"Dan." Dianne called from down near my 'office.' I hurried over to the booth in the back of the bar area and we both slid into opposite sides. She looked worried and had a couple of thin shallow lines on her forehead I'd never noticed before.

"What happened?" she asked.

Before I could answer, Shamrock hurried over and sat down beside Dianne. "I just heard you were back, Danny. What happened?"

"That didn't take long," I said. "I just got here."

"It's all we've been talking about. Now give. What's up?"

"Shamrock," Dianne said. "Is everything okay out there?" She meant the kitchen and his dishwashing duties.

"All caught up, Dianne, all caught up. Now come on, Danny, tell us what happened."

Dianne looked none too thrilled. I was nervous, almost as though an anxiety attack was coming on. I took a couple of deep breaths, sat quietly until the feeling passed.

"Well . . ." I began, fearing I might really spook Dianne. She'd only recently signed on to our little treasure hunt as it was. How she would react to this bit of information, I didn't know. There was no way out of telling her though. "He wanted to talk to me about the old coot with the fedora and topcoat."

"And . . . ?" Dianne asked warily.

"Someone trespassed in his room at the Honeymoon. Gant thought—"

"You stupid idiot," Dianne exploded, realized she spoke too loudly and continued in a tone that was softer but no less outraged. "You broke into the man's hotel room?"

"You can't really call the Honeymoon a hotel, Dianne," Shamrock said. "It's more like a—"

"Be quiet. What the hell were you thinking, Dan? Breaking into the man's home. Unbelievable."

"I didn't break in," I sputtered.

"I suppose the door was unlocked with a note on it telling you to go in and make yourself comfortable?"

I glanced at Shamrock for support. He grimaced and shrugged his shoulders almost imperceptibly.

"I wouldn't make myself comfortable in there," I said desperately. "The guy was eating . . . *dog food* up there."

I'd been hoping this treasure hunt might bring Dianne and me closer again, not drive us farther apart. Looked like I was wrong again.

"Dog food?" Shamrock said. "Ugh."

"I don't care if he's having an eight-course meal catered every day," Dianne growled. "You've got no right breaking into a man's hotel room."

"I didn't. I . . . I got a key."

"Hah!" Shamrock retorted. "You got the key from Artie? So you had permission to be in there. Then that's not so bad."

"Unfortunately, it's worse than that. He was beaten to death."

Shamrock's eyes grew so wide he looked more fish than Irish. "Sweet baby Jesus."

"God, no." Dianne groaned and covered her eyes with her hands.

They were both silent for a long time. Hopefully, both my friends considered me incapable of murder, even though they hadn't been sure about breaking and entering a minute ago.

"Beaten to death?" Shamrock finally said. "That sounds like Butchy Dunn's M.O."

"Yes, it does."

"This is just . . . wonderful," Dianne said, rubbing her forehead.

Chapter 29

AFTER LEAVING THE High Tide, I headed home. It was a dreary day on the beach and traffic was light. I stopped at Patriot's Corner for a six-pack of Heineken, crossed Ocean Boulevard, and headed down the street to my cottage.

I trudged up the stairs, unlocked the door, and heard a scuffling behind me. I didn't have time to turn around before I was bum-rushed inside. I found myself on the living room floor, the door slamming behind me.

"Get up," a voice growled.

Butchy Dunn.

I climbed to my feet as dignified as possible . . . and came face-to-face with Dunn. He apparently favored tight black T-shirts that showed off his muscles, black jeans, black sneakers, black hair, and black tattoos. He could have given Johnny Cash—the original man in black—a run for the title. The only good thing was that he didn't have a weapon in his hands. He did wear skin-tight black leather gloves.

Right behind him was the huge thug with the cauliflower ear the size of a fist. The man had a face only a mother could love, and even that was debatable. His puss looked like it had stopped more than a few haymakers in its day. He wore a maroon *Members Only* jacket. A too-small green scally cap was plopped on his large head which struck me as funny, though I didn't laugh.

"Sit down, Marlowe," Butchy snarled.

He was kind enough to direct me to my easy chair with a hard shove. I asked the question most people asked in these situations. "What do you want?"

Butchy stepped close and stared down at me. Angus stayed beside and behind him a foot or so.

"What the hell were you doing at the cop station?" Butchy demanded.

Not only was Fred Capobianco keeping an eye on me before he was murdered, it appeared I was being followed by Butchy, too—unless Fred had been reporting to Butchy. I'd known that was a possibility but with it being the off-season and not many people around, I'd assumed I would have spotted him. Obviously, I hadn't. Either Butchy Dunn had a lot of practice dodging cops and tracking down deadbeats who owed him money, or I was slipping.

Or maybe he kept an eye on the High Tide and saw me being escorted into the Hampton cruiser.

It didn't matter much now. I had a lot more to worry about.

"They wanted to ask me some questions," I answered.

"About what?"

"Some overdue traffic tickets."

The smack across my face rocked my head. I almost jumped up but thought better of it when I saw an evil grin cross Cauliflower's ugly face.

"Try again," Butchy snarled.

"They just—"

The slap this time was even harder. Cauliflower snickered.

"Again," Butchy said in a low voice. "This time forget the just."

"Okay," I said, rubbing my cheek. "It was a mistake. They—"

Another slap and the room spun in circles.

"I don't like the word mistake either," Butchy growled. "Now give me the straight dope or we'll play like this all day long. And maybe worse. My friend Angus is enjoying it. He might like to get involved."

Cauliflower's sick smile confirmed Butchy wasn't just guessing. I dreaded the thought of being slapped around by a monster like Cauliflower.

"Let me play with him for a minute, Butch. Come on, please," Cauliflower begged.

"No, Angus," Butchy said. "I want a couple of answers, then I want to wrap this up. We ain't makin' no money here. I got other things to do."

"Why don't you give me a list of the words you don't approve of first," I said. "Then maybe I can finish a complete sentence before you bitch-slap me again. And you might find out what you want to know."

I rubbed my cheek as I spoke. I never knew slaps could hurt like that. But they can, believe me, especially when they're handed out by an expert.

"You're a real funny guy, Marlowe," Butchy said, sneering at me. "But don't get too cute. You've never dealt with anyone like me before. So, give."

I kept my hand against my cheek, more for protection against another blow than to help with the stinging sensation. I picked my words carefully and hoped for the best. "They wanted to talk to me about some old coot living on the beach."

Dunn's eyebrows shot up. "Old coot? Old coot?"

"Yeah. Some old-timer who's been hanging around the beach."

"What's he look like?" Butchy asked.

"Like he came out of a Bogart movie." I barely got the words out when Butchy took another savage swipe at me. I was ready though and jerked my head back. His open hand created a breeze as it missed my cheek by an inch or two.

"Okay, okay," I said before he had a chance to try his luck again. I put my hands up in front of me. "He's probably in his eighties, wears a fedora."

"Wha's dat?" Cauliflower asked.

"Shut up, Angus," Butchy said to him. And to me, "More."

"And a topcoat."

"Who is he?" Butchy asked.

I didn't know if it was a trick question or not. Of course if it was Butchy who'd beaten Capobianco to death, as I suspected, he knew the answers already to these questions. I had to be very careful with my responses.

"Used to be a New Hampshire state cop," I said.

"And what did the cops want to ask you about him?"

"Someone killed him."

"And they thought it was you?" Butchy asked with a snicker.

"Yeah, they did."

"Why?"

"Because I was in his room."

"I know that. But what did you find?" Butchy asked.

So that was the reason for Butchy's questions. He already knew I'd been in Capobianco's room before him. Maybe he'd been watching the hotel waiting for Capobianco and saw me go in, threatened Artie the desk clerk and got the info from him. Anyway, now it appeared Butchy thought I might have found something that told the location of the gold.

"Dog food," I answered stupidly, luckily not getting slapped again.

"Dog food?" Angus asked, with an even dumber-than-usual look on his face. "What kind?"

"Shut up, stupid," Butchy snarled at his cohort, then turned back to me.

"Remember what I told you, Marlowe. If you find any-thing—including in that old fossil's hotel room—about that twenty grand, the first thing you're going to do is tell me. And don't ask how to find me. I'll find you."

This confirmed my suspicion that Butchy knew the gold was worth twenty thousand at face value and not fifteen. Or was he just playing dumb? After all, he may have been at the coin store and if so, he most likely knew the coins' real value as collectibles. Maybe he didn't think I knew their true value and was hoping to keep that fact from me. It would make sense. If I didn't know the coins' true value, Butchy prob-ably figured I might not get greedy and would be more likely to hand over to him anything I came across on the gold's location.

"A New Hampshire state cop, Butch," Angus said. "I ain't likin' dat."

"Since when have you been scared of cops, moron? He's an old man, for Chrissake."

"I know, Butch, but they still got dat warrant out on me from a couple winters ago. When me and Seamus ripped off all those copper pipes from under the cottages up here." He licked his thick lips constantly with a long, fat tongue. "The pipes was worth so much in copper that it was a felony charge, Butch, and I don't wanna go to that prison in Concord. I hear it's freezin' there. And I don't know no one there, not like I do in Walpole."

If looks could kill, Angus would be no more. "Yeah, I remember," Butchy said, "and I remember tellin' you not to get involved in any penny-ante scores with that junkie, too."

"Yeah, but it was so easy, Butch," Angus said.

"I'll easy you," Butchy said. "We gotta get goin' now." He turned back to me for hopefully the last time. "Gonna miss me, Marlowe?"

I shrugged, happy to be getting out of this visit with no more than a rosy-red cheek.

Dunn studied me for a bit, then turned to his stooge. "You want a little fun, Angus?"

A wicked grin spread across Cauliflower's face. "Sure, Butchy, sure."

"Whoa!" I held up both hands, palms out. "I told you what you wanted to know. No need for rough stuff."

Butchy smirked. "You think you're a smart guy, Marlowe. I seen plenty like you. I just wanna put an exclamation point on the end of my warning."

I was surprised Dunn knew what an exclamation point was, but I didn't have time to wonder about it.

"Just bounce him around a little, Angus," Butchy said. "Not enough for the hospital if you can help it. You know how much I hate violence. I'll be out front in the car."

Butchy snickered as he closed the door behind him. He thumped down the porch stairs.

Angus stepped up to me, reached down with his left hand and took hold of my shirt. "This won't hurt much, pretty boy." He had a sparkle in his tiny black eyes.

I glanced to my right, looking for something, anything to use as a weapon . . . and spotted a yellow number two Ticonderoga pencil sitting on the end table. I grabbed for it just as Angus was hauling me to my feet. I wrapped my hand around the eraser end and in one fast, hard move drove the pencil into the back of the hand clutching my shirt.

To my surprise, the pencil sank in deep. Angus let out a scream worse than anything I'd ever heard, a sound I never want to hear again. He dropped me and yanked his injured hand back, staring at the pencil sticking out of his hand like his slow-witted mind was trying to figure out what had happened.

I scrambled the rest of the way to my feet, gave him a shove, and raced the short distance to my bedroom. Without looking back, I dropped to my knees, reached under the bed, and pulled out Betsy. I didn't have to crack the barrel. I always kept it loaded when my kids weren't around.

When I returned to the front room, Angus was still staring at the pencil jammed into his hand. Blood dripped onto the floor. He growled, took one step toward me, and noticed the shotgun I was pointing at his stomach.

Angus cradled his injured hand. "Wait . . . hold on . . . I'm goin," he whined.

Funny how the toughest of characters will back down when there's a possibility they could be half their original height if they didn't.

Angus backed up to the door, opened it with his good hand, and took off, pencil and all, slamming down the porch stairs. I listened as a car door opened and closed. A minute later a car started, then sped toward Ocean Boulevard.

I didn't think they'd be back anytime soon, now that Butchy knew I was armed. They had to get that pencil out of Cauliflower's hand, didn't they?

I chuckled, wondering how they'd explain that to the staff at whatever hospital they ended up at. Still, I was shaking a bit. I took two Xanax from the vial in my sock drawer and washed them down with beer. Within half an hour, I was calmer. Or at least as calm as I could be, considering what I'd just been through.

Chapter 30

IT WAS EARLY evening and Shamrock and I were seated at a table near the front window of our favorite watering hole, The Crooked Shillelagh. We stayed away from the High Tide when having more than one beer because Dianne wasn't a fan of her employees indulging on premises and had banned the practice. The Shillelagh had one of the best bar atmospheres—after the Tide.

"Let's face it, Danny, we're stymied," Shamrock said. "We aren't going to find any gold. It's been too long. We have to clear you of suspicion in the old man's murder. That's more important than finding any gold."

I took a sip from my mug of Heineken. It was hard to argue with Shamrock. Still, I wasn't ready to give up on the gold. "There's got to be a way to find out if there was a Seaview cottage down near me and where exactly it was."

"You said Cora doesn't remember it. If she and her old biddy friends don't remember, I'm thinkin' no one will."

"Another beer, gents?" The young Irish barmaid, Clara, had snuck up on us. She looked the part—long red hair, blue eyes, and a sprinkle of freckles across her face. She spoke with a brogue that made Shamrock's sound like a Boston accent.

"Is the Pope Catholic, lass? You're a cute one, you are."

Clara smiled and shook her index finger at Shamrock. "Don't get fresh, Shamrock, or I'll be shutting you off."

"You'd go out of business," I said.

"Aye, that's probably true," Clara said before turning and heading toward the bar.

"Listen, Danny. Maybe it's best we drop this whole treasure hunt business. Not only am I imagining seeing Butchy Dunn every time I walk down a dark street, now you tell me that old codger who was murdered was peekin' in our damn windows. Jesus, Danny, what was that all about? He could have had our phones tapped, for all we know. Who did you say he was?"

"Fred Capobianco. An ex-state cop that I think got canned for taking bribes from the booze smugglers. That's how he might have known about the gold. If he didn't get his last payoff, he probably considered that gold rightfully his."

"What about Dunn?" Shamrock wouldn't let it go. "He threatened us; said he'd beat us silly if we didn't tell him everything we know. And he told you to keep your nose out of his business. I don't want to end up like Capo . . . whatever his name was."

Shamrock had a legitimate worry there. Butchy Dunn was a grade-A hard dude. Now that I knew his reputation— and knew that he was probably aware of the true value of the gold—I had no doubt he'd do anything to find the gold. Hadn't he just killed his own sister or ordered it done? And probably killed Capobianco, too. One or two more dead bodies to a guy like Dunn would mean less than a morning shave to some guys.

Where was Butchy anyway? On the beach or close by, I was sure.

Maybe Shamrock was right. Maybe we should get out of the whole mess. Monica was gone, after all. And she had been my main reason for looking for the gold—to help her and her son. But we might not be able drop it at this point, deep in as we were. Not if Butchy knew that we knew about the gold and its true value.

Still, I did feel an obligation to Monica's memory and to her boy, especially after meeting him. He reminded me so much of Davey. I couldn't imagine my own son growing up under those conditions. Maybe I could erase, at least in my own mind, some of the failures I'd racked up as a father. It was about time I did something for someone besides myself anyway. Helping Sam might ease my guilty conscience concerning Monica's death. I should have realized the danger we were all in. My conscience now raised my anxiety level so high sometimes that even my Xanax prescription was of little help. So to help Sam might help me, too—before it was too late and I went off the deep end again.

And then there was Dianne. I'd piqued her interest with the tale about gold and formed . . . what? A partnership? Maybe even a chance to repair our relationship? What would she think if I tried to slink out on my belly now? Not to mention that I needed money, badly—more than you can know.

I was torn between shucking the whole lousy mess and keeping on when an idea came to me out of nowhere, as ideas often do.

I must have been staring at nothing, daydreaming.

"Dan," Shamrock and Clara said at the same time.

I looked up. "Oh, sorry." I lifted my arms from the table as Clara set my beer down.

After Clara left, Shamrock asked, "What is it, Danny? You got an idea?"

"What makes you think that?" I asked, not really expecting an answer.

"First of all, you were in some type of hypnotic trance when Clara brought our beers. Second—and this is the proof in the pudding—you didn't check out the lassie's nice caboose like you always do when she sashays away from our table."

I smiled, took a sip of the new beer. "Very perceptive, Shamrock. You're good."

"I know," Shamrock said, beaming. Then he fell dead serious. "Come on, Danny, give. Tell me."

I told Shamrock my idea. It offered only an outside chance, but was possible, or so I believed.

Shamrock must have had the same opinion because he said, "Ahhh, Danny, my boy, you are good."

"It's a long shot, but better than nothing, and I don't see what we've got to lose except . . ." I hesitated.

"What is it, Danny?

"It might be very time-consuming. We'll most likely need more hands and eyes."

Shamrock's face collapsed in a frown. "Jesus, Danny, please. Don't say it . . . I beg you. Don't say those names."

I didn't want to, but we needed help with my plan, and the last thing we wanted to do was tell anybody new about our little secret.

Shamrock saw the answer in my face and shook his head in resignation.

Chapter 31

WE MOVED TO my green Chevette, still 'discussing' the matter as I headed to the Tide to pick up Dianne. Shamrock sat beside me, still in his restaurant whites. Dianne climbed in the back, dressed casually in blue shorts and a red t-shirt.

"For the love of all that's holy," Shamrock grumbled for the hundredth time. "Do we really need them? Can't we do it ourselves?"

We were heading down Route 1A. When we reached O'Keefe's Store, we turned right on to Route 286.

"When you see this place," I said, "you'll know why we need all the help we can get."

"I just wish you'd told me before I got in the car that you were picking them up," Dianne said. "I'm swapping seats with you as soon as we stop, Shamrock. I'm not being jammed back here with those two creeps."

Shortly after I reached Seabrook, I took a right turn into a mobile home park. The homes were of upscale quality and the grounds perfectly landscaped. I followed the twists and turns of the road until I came to a cul-de-sac and stopped in front of a small but well-kept mobile home. I beeped the horn once. Two slats in a window blind opened an inch and quickly closed.

"Remember," I said quickly, "they think there's only fifteen thousand in gold, not gold coins. Don't mention the real amount, no matter what you do."

"Wouldn't Butchy Dunn have told them, if he knows?" Shamrock asked.

"They're the last two people anyone, including Dunn, would tell about a million dollars' worth of gold," I answered. "It's bad enough they know about the twenty grand . . . here they come."

Two men came out the front door and headed toward the car.

"I wonder why Butchy told them anything?" Shamrock asked.

"He probably thought they could help find it," I said. "He doesn't know the beach, remember? And Eddie snowed him about being 'the man' down here. Do you really think Dunn ever would have handed them one coin of that treasure?"

"I guess not," Shamrock said.

Dianne and Shamrock got out of the car and changed seats.

Eddie slid into the middle rear seat beside Shamrock who was behind me against the rear door. Derwood crawled in after Eddie and slammed the door.

"Hey, everybody. How's it going?" Eddie Hoar said, smacking gum.

"Good, Eddie," I answered. Shamrock grunted; Dianne said nothing.

"Hello," said Derwood Doller.

"Hi, Derwood," I said.

"Dianne Dennison," Eddie said excitedly. "Gee, I ain't seen you since——"

"Since she barred you from the High Tide for skipping on your check," Shamrock said.

"Well . . . well . . . um . . . that was just a misunderstanding," Eddie said. "I thought I paid before I left."

"Ha, sure you did," Shamrock said. "That's why you almost killed an entire bottle of Dianne's most expensive cognac before you split. You never drink that stuff. You drink the cheapest bar booze we have."

Eddie guffawed. "Always joking, Shamrock. You're the best, my friend."

Shamrock's voice lowered. "I'm not joking and I'm not your friend."

"Yeah, yeah," Eddie said, nodding and blinking rapidly. "But you're not holding any hard feelings, are you, Dianne? You got paid, right?"

Dianne turned to glare at Eddie. "After I . . . I mean Dan . . . had to chase you all over the beach."

"But I paid," Eddie offered. "So everything's hunky-dory now, right?"

"I'll hunky-dory you," Shamrock growled.

I drove the car down the twisty road out of the mobile home park and headed back toward Hampton Beach.

"Have you guys seen Butchy Dunn?" I asked. I could see Eddie's face in the rearview. He gulped hard at the mention of Butchy's name.

He answered, "Nope, and I hope we never do."

"I knew you'd be trying to avoid him," I said. "That's why I gave you a call at your aunt's. You always seem to hide out there when you're in trouble."

"Harrumph!" Shamrock said. "You might as well move in permanently."

"Ha, Ha," Eddie said nervously.

"Yeah, Dan," Derwood said. "Eddie really got us in a jackpot this time. This Dunn's a crazy man. I asked around— he's bad news. Worse than I even thought."

"Whattaya mean, I got us in this jackpot?" Eddie said. "What the hell did I do? I didn't ask him to come up here and look for no . . . no gold."

"You blabbed when you were in the joint together," Derwood said. "Otherwise he wouldn't have any interest in us. I told ya before you went in to keep your big mouth shut and do your time. But, nooooooo, you had to shoot off your mouth. You have to be the big wheel. Now look where we are."

"Look, Dumwood, if it wasn't for me, you'd—"

"I told you not to call me that," Derwood interrupted. "Especially today. I'm on a short leash."

Derwood hooked his left arm around Eddie's neck, got him in a headlock, and started rubbing a knuckle noogie hard on Eddie's skull.

Eddie howled.

I swerved the car and glared in my rearview mirror. "Knock it off you two or I'll pull over here. You can get out and no two hundred dollars."

"Both of you," Shamrock yelled. "Knock it off."

Dianne turned, watching the scene in the back seat. "Stop it, you two idiots, or you'll never set foot in my restaurant again."

That seemed to do the trick. Derwood was a fan of our baked haddock and ordered it every time he came . . . when he wasn't banned along with Eddie, that is.

Derwood stopped. Eddie rubbed his head, patted down his wrinkled purple disco shirt. His flushed face accentuated his pockmarks somehow.

"Oh, come on, can't ya take a joke for Chrissake?" Eddie said.

"Not from you," Derwood said sullenly. "Not today."

Shamrock snickered. Dianne turned back to the front.

"By the way," Eddie said. "When are we gonna get that two hundred bucks?"

"When hell freezes over, if I had my way," Shamrock said.

"When we find what we're looking for," I said, glancing at Eddie and Derwood in the rearview. I wondered if I'd made the right decision to bring them along on this trip. I hadn't had many options. We did need more eyes, and the last thing I wanted was to have more folks knowing about the gold. So, I was stuck with the two knuckleheads behind me.

"At the house?" Eddie asked quickly. "You'll pay us then?"

"Good try, Eddie," I said. "I told you on the phone you'd get it when, and if, we find the thing we're looking for."

"The gold." Eddie shook his small head. "That's another thing, Dan. Twenty k in gold. We're only gettin' two hundred bucks? It don't seem right."

"I'm fine with it," Derwood said. "I don't want to be involved in this any more than I already am." Derwood looked sourly at Eddie. "Thanks to you."

"You're lucky you're getting that, Eddie," I said. "You fingered me to Butchy, wrecked my house, and got my head almost smashed in."

"Yeah," Shamrock said angrily. "If I had my way, I'd stop the car and give you a good thumping and leave you in a ditch where you belong. I still haven't forgotten that shit show you almost got me and Dan killed over last year."

Shamrock was talking about an unpleasant experience with some unsavory characters he and I had become mixed up with through no fault of our own. Eddie bore the fault for that one.

"Well, you're all right, ain't you?" Eddie asked.

"No thanks to you," Shamrock answered.

We'd traveled back across the bridge into Hampton Beach, traversed the strip over to Winnacunnet Road, took a right at the end, and were headed north on Route One. I took a left at the light at The Old Salt Restaurant, and another left not too long after that. I passed a few homes and pulled the car to the curb.

"This is it?" Dianne asked. She stared, open mouthed, out her side window.

"Yup." I nodded.

Shamrock craned his neck, peering around Eddie to get a better view. "Christ, if I was a landscaper, I could make a killing here."

The house, what you could see of it, was a yellow ranch-style with more peeled-off paint spots than not. The yard looked like it had been neglected since the beginning of time. Out-of-control shrubs and bushes completely covered large parts of the house, growing up to the roof in spots. The grass, if that was what it was, was a good foot high.

"Holy shit. What's it look like inside?" Derwood asked.

"Stop bellyaching," I said. "Let's go in and do what we came to do."

Chapter 32

AFTER WADING THROUGH the overgrown lawn and pushing aside bushes that semi-blocked the entranceway, I gave the front door a good beating. I didn't bother with the doorbell, assuming it suffered the same neglect as the lawn and was unlikely to work.

We stood huddled there, the five of us, for about a minute. Finally, the door opened, revealing a man with thick, long, white hair and a similar beard. He wore a red flannel shirt with matching suspenders that held up gray wool pants and had a round, jovial face that could have belonged to Santa Claus.

"Dan Marlowe," he said in a deep voice. "Come in, come on in."

He moved out of the way, and we all squeezed inside. And when I say squeezed, I mean squeezed. We found ourselves in a tiny foyer. On either side, in two adjoining rooms, were piles of what looked like bound newspapers, magazines, and every type of ephemera you could think of. The place smelled like the basement of a library after a flood.

The piles went from floor almost to the ceiling. My companions glanced around in awe. Me not so much. I'd been here before.

"How've you been, Zach?" I asked.

"Fine, Dan, can't complain. You still got the cards up at the High Tide?" He was referring to the postcards I'd bought from him years ago when I first purchased the Tide. There were dozens, all depicting old-time scenes of Hampton Beach. I'd had them framed, and they still adorned the restaurant walls. Gave the patrons something to look at while they were waiting for a table on a busy evening.

"They're still there," I answered.

"I see you brought some help." Zach gave the group a once-over. "You'll need them, considering what you said you're looking for."

I made introductions all the way around.

"Follow me," Zach said. He turned and headed along a pathway with towering piles of newspapers and boxes on either side. We followed. I actually had to turn sideways to make it past a couple of very tight spots.

"What a dump," Eddie muttered behind me.

"Shut up, Eddie," I said softly over my shoulder.

We gathered into a small hallway at the end of the paper tunnel. We were so close, I could smell everyone's breath, which did not diminish the smell of old, musty paper that permeated the house.

"Okay," Zach said, his face beaming. He jerked his thumb toward a door on the right. "Over there we got everything north of the Casino including North Beach. And there," he turned his thumb to a door on the left, "is what you want . . . everything south of the Casino."

"What's that?" Eddie asked, nodding at a door directly in front of us.

"The head," Zach said.

"Yeah, that's what I want," Eddie exclaimed. He wormed his way around us and into the bathroom. "You mind, Zach?" He asked as he closed the door behind him.

"Help yourself," Zach said.

I heard Eddie lock the door . . . I didn't like that.

Zach opened the door that led to the room on the left.

Shamrock let out a low whistle. "Sweet Mother Mary."

The small room was like the room we'd just passed through—covered floor to almost ceiling with boxes, magazines, newspapers, and what have you.

"Everything in there is about Hampton Beach?" Dianne asked.

"Just the south beach," Zach answered with pride. A moment later he added, "You're lucky you didn't want anything about the town. That's all downstairs and there's a lot of it, too. You might not like the smell down there. A little musty."

As if on cue, Derwood let out a sneeze so loud I jumped.

Zach let out a deep belly laugh. "Yeah, the air can do that until you're used to it like me."

I didn't know if I could ever get used to a place like this. My nose was beginning to itch. Where did Zach sleep? On top of a pile of newspapers?

Zach got out of the way, jamming his bulk against a wall and sucking in his ample belly. "Knock yourselves out," he said. "Just one thing I ask. Please keep everything in order, like you find it. I've got it all catalogued pretty good."

I didn't know if he was kidding or not, so I quickly asked, "Anything about a Seaview cottage back in the day?"

He shook his head slowly. "Sorry, Dan, I'm not that good. All I can tell you is if it's in my house, it's in this room. Better than that, I can't do. Good hunting. I've got cataloguing to do."

I went into the room first, wandering down a tight passage through the towering piles. Dianne was behind me, then Derwood, followed by Shamrock. A few piles were shorter than the rest, about waist high. Maybe used as makeshift tables by people going through the debris like we were about to do? Anyway, I decided that's what we'd use the shorter piles for too. I went to a window at the far wall almost totally obscured by boxes. The rest of the gang spread out behind me.

"What's taking Eddie so long?" I asked, looking at Derwood. I don't know why I asked. I already knew.

I assumed Zach was wise enough not to keep any controlled drugs in his medicine cabinet, especially since he let all sorts of people go through his paper collection. That was his business, after all. He made his living selling Hampton Beach ephemera, although I assumed it was a supplement to a pension or Social Security or both. But who knew? With someone like him and a racket like this? He could be a millionaire, for all I knew.

Before Derwood could respond, the bathroom door opened, and Eddie strolled out. He came in behind Shamrock and surveyed the room with eyes that I could see were pinned even from where I stood. He smacked his gum and said, "This is gonna cost you more than two bills, Dan, my man."

Shamrock spun to face him. "Bullshit, you eejit. You'll take what you agreed to and like it. If I'm stuck working beside you, you'll be lucky if I don't slam a bundle of newspapers on your empty head."

Eddie held up his hands. "Okay, Irish, okay. Just kidding."

"I don't like your kidding. And don't call me Irish. The name's Mister Kelly to the likes of you." Shamrock did a double take on Eddie's eyes. "Jesus, Mary, and Joe. This damn fool's high as a goddamn kite."

I rolled my eyes. "Well, if it's speed, maybe he'll be able to put in some real work for a change."

"Just don't crowd me, Eddie. I'm warning you." Shamrock shook a scarred fist in Eddie's face.

"Take it easy, Irish ... ahh ... Mister Kelly." Eddie snickered and blushed.

"That's better," Shamrock said, nodding firmly.

"All right," I announced. "Let's get going. You all know what we're looking for—old beach cottages on the sand. You find anything, hand it to me." I glanced at Eddie. "And remember, Eddie, put everything back where it goes. The postcards are our best bet. Everyone grab a stack and start searching."

⇦   ⇨

"YOU DIRTY THIEF!"

The five of us had been going through paper for over an hour when Shamrock shouted from the other end of the room. I squeezed by Dianne and Derwood and waded through paper to find my Irish friend had Eddie pushed up against a stack of newspapers and was holding him by his shirt collar, shaking him violently.

Eddie's face was flushed and his eyes bugged.

"What's wrong?" I asked.

"This bloody highwayman is stealing postcards, Danny," Shamrock said, giving Eddie's shirt a vicious tug as he did. "Stuffing them in his pockets. I saw him."

"Give, Eddie," I said, holding out my hand. We were jammed in so close my fingers almost touched Eddie's scrawny chest.

Eddie snaked his hand behind him and came out with a few old postcards from his rear pant pocket.

I took the postcards and gave Eddie what I hoped was a threatening look. "That all of them?"

"Give them all, you son of a serpent," Shamrock snarled. He poked Eddie so hard with his index finger, I thought he'd drill a hole in Eddie's chest.

"Okay . . . okay," Eddie squeaked. He dug more postcards from his other rear pocket and handed them to me. "Jeez, it was only a few postcards . . . and look at the shit this nut has here. He won't ever miss them. Besides, Dan, you're only giving us the two balloons to go through all this shit. My asthma is startin' to kick up again. Can't blame a guy for tryin' to subsidize his meager pay."

"I'll subsidize you," Shamrock roared, cocking his right fist as Eddie cowered and let out a squeal a pig would be proud of.

I grabbed Shamrock's arm. "He's not worth it. Zach was good enough to let us go through this unattended and I don't want him to hear us arguing. We might have to come back sometime and all this might shake his trust."

Shamrock sputtered and let go of Eddie's shirt.

"Mess up again, Eddie, and I'm going to let Shamrock have his way with you," I said. "Or maybe I'll let Butchy know where you're hiding out."

Eddie's eyes widened. "You wouldn't do that, would you, Dan?"

I tipped my head. "Maybe. Maybe not. Just don't tempt me, Eddie. Steal again, and Shamrock and I'll both bounce you around. So smarten up."

I gave Eddie a little push in the direction of the pile he was supposed to be working on.

None of this came as a surprise. The surprise would have been if Eddie hadn't tried to lift anything. Stealing was as natural to Eddie as robbing eggs was for a weasel. Just the nature of the creature. The best you could do was try and control his thievery. With Eddie, that control came through fear. Fear that Shamrock and I would beat him bloody or Butchy Dunn would do worse. After getting caught, and Shamrock threatening to tear off his head, I was fairly certain Eddie wouldn't attempt any more theft today. Not while he was under Shamrock's eagle eye, anyway.

I squished myself past Derwood over to Dianne. I started to pass her when she said softly, "Dan, look at this."

She handed me a beat-up ancient postcard, ragged around the edges. I strained to make out the image but couldn't.

I scanned the card with a magnifying glass that Zach apparently left around for customers and saw it appeared to have never been sent through the mail. The card featured a wide-shot photograph that looked like a family—father, mother and three children. They were posed in front of a cottage. The clothes they all wore suggested an early 1900s timeframe, but that was just a guess. I struggled to make out the letters on the sign behind the family, hanging from the overhang above the porch.

S...e...a...v...i...e... the rest was obscured, but it was enough.

This had to be it.

There may have been other Seaview cottages on Hampton Beach, but I had a gut feeling this was what I was looking for. The area looked different from today, but I sensed this was the "Island" section of the beach. I could almost make out the side of a building, off in the distance, on what I believed to be Ocean Boulevard.

What street the photo had been taken on, I couldn't be sure. We'd work on that later. The street was unpaved—I could see that. But most were back then, or so I assumed.

I grabbed Dianne by the shoulders, pulled her close, and gave her a quick kiss. She gave me a little half-smile, but didn't knock me on my ass, and that was good.

Derwood asked, "You two find something?"

"I don't think so," I said, reluctant to let him and Eddie know what she'd found.

"What? What?" Eddie shouted. The man rarely missed a trick and his hustler radar must have vibrated. He shimmied his way over to us, followed by Shamrock.

"Let's see. Let's see." Eddie held out his hand for the card.

There was no way in hell I was going to let Eddie Hoar know any more than he already did, which was already too much. Sure, I'd used Eddie and Derwood to help us plow through this mountain of paper, but I'd been desperate.

I'd visited Zach before and knew the huge amount of junk straining the seams of his house. Even though I wasn't completely sure that this postcard showed the cottage I was looking for, it was probable enough I planned to keep the postcard far from Eddie's eyes. If I didn't and it was the Real McCoy, Eddie would be down on the beach with a shovel faster than a starving seagull swooping down on a peanut butter and jelly sandwich on a vacant beach blanket.

"Not today," I said to Eddie, winking at Shamrock over his shoulder.

"Whattaya mean, not today?" Eddie whined. "We did our part. We helped. Ain't that right, Derwood?"

Derwood shrugged. "I told you Eddie . . . I don't want to be involved with anything having to do with Butchy Dunn. Dan said he'd pay us if he finds what he's looking for. That's good enough for me. I just wanna live."

"You moron," Eddie sputtered. "You'd screw up free lunch and go back for the change. This could a been my big score."

Turning back to me, Eddie cooed, "Let me just take a quick look, Dan, out of professional curiosity."

I chuckled. "Nice try again, Eddie, but I think I'll keep this to myself for now."

Eddie grumbled something I couldn't make out.

"Okay, let's put everything back like we found it," I said. "It's starting to get dark and I think we're all getting tired anyway."

There were collective nods around the room.

After we'd returned everything as best we could, I called out to Zach, who trudged up from his cellar. The musty odor came up with him.

"Find what you were looking for, Dan?" Zach asked.

"I think so."

"Good, good," Zach said, seeming genuinely happy he had a satisfied customer. I showed Zach the stack of old postcards I held. He took them and counted them. Dianne and I had taken out an occasional card as we'd gone along, cards we thought would add to the decor at the High Tide. And even though the price he mentioned seemed like peanuts to me, he seemed pleased with the sale. I felt better paying for the stack than if we'd walked out with just one card after all the time we'd spent going through his stock.

I paid Zach and thanked him for his hospitality, then we slithered our way through the house and out the front door.

Chapter 33

IT WAS EARLY evening. I dropped everyone off and drove home. Once inside, I took out the postcard and studied it closely. Without a magnifying glass, it was difficult to see what I'd already determined was there, let alone anything new. I decided to take the card to the one person who might be able to pinpoint the location.

I walked from my cottage to Cora Petit's home. She wasn't out on the porch, so I went up the few stairs and rapped on the front door.

Within a few minutes, Cora opened the door. "Oh, Daniel. How are you? Please, do come in."

Cora stepped out of the way, and I walked into her front room. It was like stepping into a time machine set fifty years in the past. The decor was something my elderly aunt had favored in her home before she passed. Maybe not favored as much as she neglected to update the decor for one reason or another, like Cora had. Financial reasons, maybe. Or maybe older people just grow comfortable with what they are used to.

"Have a seat, Daniel."

I took the chair she indicated, a comfortable rocker with flowered upholstery and matching arms. It squeaked as I sat.

"I was just about to have some tea and cookies. Would you like some?"

I had a stronger beverage in mind, but I knew Cora didn't partake. Besides, I was sure she'd heard stories about my overindulgence in the past, and I wanted to preserve the semi-straight persona I was trying to project. "Thanks, Cora, that would be nice."

Cora shuffled off to the kitchen and I studied the room. The walls, which were knotty pine like my own place, were festooned with framed photographs. Pictures of people out of another era, most of them at the beach—during a time when Hampton Beach was in its infancy.

I noticed a sense of satisfaction on the faces of the men and women in the old photos. And why not? The land was leased for a pittance, either by themselves or with a relative or partner, one of the many 5,000-square-foot cookie-cutter lots the town had offered in the early days to stimulate interest in the beach. Many working- and middle-class people jumped at the chance to have a second home on the seashore. Folks came from Manchester in New Hampshire, Lowell and Lawrence in Massachusetts, and as far south as Woburn, which was just a dozen miles north of Boston.

The lessees had, in almost all cases, jammed two structures on the lots, there being few, if any, zoning laws back then. Their partner and/or relatives would have one cottage while they took the other. If there was no partner, the second cottage would be rented out and the proceeds used to pay for the construction of the buildings, upkeep, and any bills. Profit from the rental of the second unit came about fairly quickly as the new summer destination caught on. Adding to the pride of ownership, many of the buildings were built by the lessees themselves, the pioneers of Hampton Beach. That accounted for the lack of similarity from cottage to cottage. They'd been built by a thousand different hands.

I drifted for a bit, thinking of what an exciting time it must have been on the beach back in those days. Everything new and wide open.

All that was threatened today. Although the beach was still my home, it was changing yearly. For the better, many said. But others disagreed. I wasn't sure who was right. I assumed time would tell. Hampton appeared to be turning into a destination that only the well-off would be able to afford, and that wouldn't be the Hampton Beach I'd known and loved through the years.

Can't the rich leave us anything? I wondered. Apparently not or so it looked to me. And there was nothing I could do to hold back that change. If I was even here to see it and not in jail or dead by the hand of Butchy Dunn before then.

Cora bustled back into the room carrying a silver serving tray. I didn't know if it was real silver or not and didn't care. On the tray were dainty china cups. Like the tray, I didn't know if they were real china or not. I don't know much about those things. Cora set the serving tray down on the small, dark wood table with claw legs directly in front of me. She poured tea into the two cups, both with pink rose designs, and sat on the sofa opposite me.

"How do you like your tea, Daniel?" she asked.

I had no idea. "However you're having it, Cora."

There didn't seem to be much of a choice, there being only one pitcher of what looked like cream as she poured a spot into both of our cups and used small tongs to place one sugar cube in each of our cups. None of the poisonous artificial stuff I preferred was in sight.

She handed a cup to me. There were spoons for stirring, which I did.

"Help yourself to the cookies, Daniel," she said, motioning to a perfectly arranged group of cookies—sugar, if I had to guess—laid out on a matching plate. I took one of the tiny cookies and nibbled at it. I assumed Cora rarely got the opportunity to use her silver and china living by herself. Suddenly, I realized how alone she must be. I nodded in appreciation as the cookie disappeared in two bites. If I'd been elsewhere, I could have demolished it in one bite, but I felt obligated to show my host appreciation for this fancy setup.

"Delicious," I said. "Thank you."

Cora smiled. "I'm glad you like them . . . I made them myself."

She took a sip of her tea, as I did, then set the cup back on the table. I felt a little odd holding the dainty little cup in my hand. The tea tasted good but there wasn't enough caffeine, I knew, to get the jolt I usually needed at this time of day. I had to remember to have a Diet Coke when I returned home.

Cora's eyes sparkled and she placed her hands together. "All right, Daniel. Please don't keep me waiting. I'm anxious to know why you're here. Have you learned some new things about our beach and its history?"

I removed the postcard from the inside pocket of my jacket and handed it across the table to her. She took it in her hands, her skin thin as paper. She wore no glasses but studied the photo without any sign of strain. It dawned on me that she most likely wouldn't be able to make out any-thing without an aid such as the magnifying glass I'd used at Zach's. I didn't need to worry, though. Apparently, Cora's sturdy French stock had gifted her with excellent eyesight, even into her later years.

"Oh, good Lord!" Cora whispered, one hand going to her mouth.

I leaned forward, my arms on my knees. "You recognize something?"

"Oh my . . . of course I do." She regained her com-posure and held the photo between bony fingers, using the index finger of her other hand to point at the picture.

"That's my Aunt Emma and Uncle Durant and my won-derful cousins." Her eyes misted. "All gone now. I've never seen this picture, Daniel. Where did you get it?"

"From a postcard collector."

"What a treasure," she said. "It was popular back then to have photographs made into postcards. I do remember that. People would send them to friends and relatives to show them what a wonderful time they were having at our beach."

"Do you know where they are in the picture, Cora?" I asked breathlessly.

"Certainly, Daniel. That has to be the cottage lost in the hurricane of '38. I can tell by what I can see around it."

"The Seaview?"

"I don't remember if that was the name," she answered, still gazing at the photo, eyes moist.

"The sign does say Seaview, Cora. But you don't remem-ber any Seaview?"

She shook her head slowly. "No, I don't." She gazed off for a bit as if trying to pull up a long-lost memory.

"In the beginning," she finally said, "it was Father and my Uncle Durant who built the two cottages. My aunt and uncle had the one in back for a couple of years. Then Uncle Durant had a problem. I'm not sure what . . . . maybe the drink. They may have rented this one for a summer, but I can't remember for sure."

A slight blush came to her cheeks. "Mother and Father never spoke of it. My aunt and uncle had to sell. Because both cottages were on one lot, there was no one who wanted to buy a property with a partner they didn't know. I'm sure my folks didn't want to worry about sharing the properties and all that entails, either. So my parents bought it. They borrowed the money and quickly rented it out to cover the loan."

"But the Seaview name?" I asked again gingerly. I didn't want to insult Cora's memory, but I had to ask, "You don't remember if it was named the Seaview?"

"Well . . . let me see," she began. "It must have been when my aunt and uncle owned it. I wasn't here for a few years. I was at Lowell Teacher's College. I lived in Lowell with other young ladies and worked there as a clerk in the summers. I did come here occasionally but never heard the name of the cottage." She blushed a bit. "Or I could have forgotten it."

This was all great news, but there was one more thing that bothered me. "Your cottage faces this way, toward the street, Cora. The photo shows them standing in front of the Seaview, and it appears they—and the cottage—are facing the ocean. Are you sure it's the same place?"

"You know how close the cottages are around here, Daniel. Back then my mother heard complaints from tenants that they didn't enjoy sitting on their porch and not being able to see the ocean. So Mother decided to move the cottage over to give the back building a clear view of the water. That way they could get higher ocean view rents right away. They really didn't tell me all that much, Daniel. I'm just surmising that's how it was. I was pretty young after all."

"I think you're surmising correctly," I said. "It all makes sense."

Cora let out a hearty laugh. "Like I said, I wasn't here for a couple of summers. I just remember Mother being adamant about the back cottage having a clear ocean view so they could get a higher rental price. Mother made Father do the project on weekends, I think. She knew the value of a dollar and, I think, she browbeat the poor man into doing it. He didn't have much free time. It likely took a few summers before he rebuilt this camp and the back camp lost its ocean view."

Then it dawned on me. "You mean this cottage wasn't here for some time . . . and the Seaview had an ocean view for awhile?"

"Yes, but for how long I don't know."

So, there it was. The cottage the bootleggers had rented. But if the shootout was at the Beach Wind, then known as the Seaview, Cora would had to have known about it, either from her parents or other locals, wouldn't she?

So I decided to ask, diplomatically. "One more thing, Cora. It's important. For my research on the book. Did you ever hear of anything bad happening in the Beach Wind, back when it was the Seaview?"

She handed the photo back to me. "Oh, Daniel. I don't want to lie to you," she said, wringing her hands like she was washing them. "Would you promise not to put this in your book if I tell you something?"

Seeing there was no book planned, that was an easy request. "Of course, Cora. I promise."

Cora proceeded to tell me about the shootout between the bootleggers and cops. Nothing that I didn't already know, but somehow more interesting coming from her.

When she finished, I asked, "Why didn't you want to tell me this, Cora?"

"Well, Daniel," she said, wringing her hands so hard I thought they might rip. "My father never wanted to advertise the horrible thing that happened there. He said people would be afraid to rent the cottage. How could you relax and have a proper vacation if you know a violent incident . . ." She shuddered, then continued, ". . . a violent incident like that had taken place. People would shy away. Like Father, I rarely mentioned the terrible story."

That made perfect sense. Today a story like that was more likely to be a positive attraction for renters or buyers. Notoriety adds value in the modern world. But back in the day, when the happening was fresh, it would have deterred prospective renters.

Cora could have told me the story of the shootout the first day I'd inquired, but I didn't begrudge her that. She was old school and had a right to her feelings.

I'd found out all I could from the photo. I finished my now-cold tea, gave Cora the postcard, and left. I was closer to finding the treasure if there really was a treasure. I just hoped no one else was as close.

Chapter 34

SHAMROCK AND I met at Clew's Hardware, an iconic business not far from Shamrock's place. I held the screen door open as we both walked into the old wooden building. To the right was a room full of beds, mattresses, and other inexpensive furniture, all ideal for a landlord to furnish a rental cottage. In front of us was a long counter with every screw, nut, bolt, and fastener known to man.

Clew's was the go-to place for anything a beach resident would need for a minor repair. An added benefit was that you didn't have to leave the beach to get whatever you needed. With the heavy traffic we get during the summer months, this was a big plus.

We'd barely reached the counter when a man greeted us. "Dan, Shamrock. Haven't seen you two in a while."

He was tall with salt and pepper hair, one of the two brothers, Jay and Fred, who, along with their sister, ran the store. But I wasn't sure which of the brothers was which.

"Both been working a lot at the Tide," I said.

"Glad to hear you're back behind the bar, Dan," the man said. "I'll have to drop by for a cold one and say 'hi'."

"Any time," I replied.

"What can I do for you gentlemen?" Jay or Fred glanced at the furniture. "I just got a shipment of new mattresses . . . top quality, firm, and you'll sleep like a baby. No sore back with these beauties. Give you a ten-percent discount 'cause they just came in. Need room for some recliners comin' in next week."

"Not today," I said.

Jay—I was almost certain this brother was Jay—looked disappointed.

I hurriedly continued, "We could use some other big items though."

Jay brightened up, probably pleased that we weren't there for just a matching nut and bolt. "Okay," he said. "What can I get you?"

"Three shovels," I answered.

"And a metal detector," Shamrock piped in.

Jay put his hand to his forehead. "Jesus Christ! Is there treasure down on the beach or something?"

Shocked, I tried to cover our tracks. "No. I lost my high school class ring somewhere around my cottage and we're hoping to find it."

Jay looked embarrassed. "I wasn't being nosy. It's just that a couple of other gents were in here getting the same thing a couple days back."

"Metal detector, too?" Shamrock asked.

"Bingo," Jay answered, "and they didn't look like metal detector hobbyists, that's for sure."

Even though I didn't want to pique his curiosity, I had to ask, "What did they look like?"

"Like they were on work release from Concord State Prison."

I glanced at Shamrock to find him staring at me, eyes wide.

"Anything else you can tell us?" I asked.

"They paid in cash. That's all I care about," Jay said. "Hold on a sec, I'll get your stuff."

"Better throw in one of the longest tape measures you got, too," I said.

He hurried into a rear room and a minute later was back with two short-handled shovels, a metal detector with a sand sifter hanging from it, and a large tape measure.

"Can we put it on account?" I asked.

"Whose?" Jay asked, a blush coming into his cheeks.

"Put it on mine," Shamrock offered.

Jay seemed relieved. "No problem."

As I've mentioned before, once you ruin your reputation in a small town like Hampton, it takes a long time to rebuild. Apparently, my rep needed a bit more time . . . at least at Clew's Hardware.

I took the metal detector and tape measure; Shamrock grabbed the three shovels. We said goodbye and stepped outside into the warm sunshine. The wind blowing off the water was chilly, though.

"Dunn and his damn Irish thug got here before us," Shamrock said, his eyes squinting in the sun.

"No doubt," I said.

Shamrock's eyes opened wide. "We've got to get digging, then. Get the you-know-what before they do."

"Don't panic," I said. "Remember, he doesn't know exactly where it is. We can assume that he knew it was one-hundred yards from the front of the Seaview. But he may not know where the Seaview was. If it wasn't for Cora Petit and

Zach's old postcards, we wouldn't know. And as far as the piles go, it's unlikely he'd decipher that little clue. Before this, the closest Dunn's ever been to Hampton Beach was probably Lawrence to load up his dope distributors."

Shamrock's tension seemed to ease. "You're right there. Still . . . we have to get a move on. Butchy bought all the right equipment, so we don't want to find ourselves digging beside him . . . and . . . and . . . Angus."

"There's one more thing, Shamrock. If we are right about the location of the gold, we're going to need help lugging it up to my cottage."

"Your cottage?"

"It's close. That'll likely be as far as we can drag it anyway."

"Why?"

"If we're right about the number of coins, they might weigh close to one thousand pounds. Besides the fact my place is the closest, we can hide it *under* the cottage. I've got those ground-level doors."

"Sweet baby Jesus," Shamrock said, slapping his forehead with an open palm. "I forgot about that."

"We'll need at least two other men."

"Two!" Shamrock shook his head vigorously. "Not Hoar and Derwood. They'll tell the whole beach."

"Who then?"

Shamrock snapped his fingers. "I'll get two of my countrymen from down in Irish Town."

'Irish Town' was in a street off Ashworth Avenue where most of the summer help from Ireland stayed each season.

"Can we trust them?" I asked.

Shamrock nodded. "I know a couple who will keep their mouths shut, even when they're in their cups."

"Even if it's gold?" I asked.

"They won't say a word. I got them over here for the summer and they want to stay. They know I can make that happen. Besides, we don't have to tell them it's gold."

"What then?" I asked.

"Danny boy, you have such little faith. If the luck of the Irish isn't shining on us now, it never will be. Something will turn up, don't worry."

"Okay," I said, hoping Shamrock was right about the luck of the Irish.

Chapter 35

A FEW DAYS later, around midnight, Shamrock and I were down on the beach with our treasure-hunting equipment. The only sound was that of waves breaking on the shore.

Shamrock had brought two friends, Sean and Connor, who both looked like they had the map of Ireland on their faces. Their brogues were so thick, I had trouble understanding them. Both were tall and wiry but looked like they each could lift a beer keg by themselves.

Fortunately, there was no moon out and because of the season, no lights on in nearby cottages. Except for our little group, the beach was deserted.

Shamrock and I had used the tape measure to find a spot about three hundred feet from where we hoped the front porch of the Seaview had stood over half a century ago. We started using the metal detector at the beginning of a small piece of rotted piles that protruded from the sand.

Shamrock had commandeered the metal detector. Since he had used one before and I was a novice, I was fine with that.

He moved slowly outward and away from the rotting pile, waving the metal detector above the sand a few inches.

Occasionally, the instrument would beep softly. Except for the sound of our slow footsteps and the low-tide waves lapping against the shore, the beach was deathly quiet and the machine's beeps sounded like Big Ben chiming.

Hoping no one else could hear the beeps, I glanced around. All I could see in any direction was an occasional seagull heading out to sea for a late-night snack.

More than once, Shamrock stopped and used the sand sifter to see what caused the machine to beep. He found a few beer caps but nothing of value.

Shamrock had moved out about fifty feet from the edge of the piles and was still waving the detector wand over the sand when the detector started beeping like the driver of a runaway car.

I moved to his side. Shamrock maneuvered the device until he got the strongest reaction.

"Okay, boys, let's start here," he said to his two Irish friends. We began digging with the shovels we got at Clew's.

I had no idea what Sean and Connor thought we were looking for. Shamrock, being the first to immigrate from Ireland to Hampton many years ago, had helped countless others from Ireland come to our beach through the years. How he did it, I had no idea. But these two fellows had asked no questions as far as I knew.

Within minutes, Connor's shovel hit something metal with a loud scraping noise. The three of us dug furiously.

I had no idea what the gold would be contained in if we found it. Shamrock and I had talked about this. We'd been sure it would have to be something sturdy to withstand the corrosive salt water that seeped through the sand over the years. We had been worried that the bootleggers might have buried it in a container that would have resisted destruction, something other than metal. That would have made our metal detector useless.

Thankfully for us, it looked like the gold had been buried in a metal box of some kind. Shamrock took over from Sean and moved in beside me. We dug around the object, uncovering a long, rectangular shape. When the object was almost fully visible, Connor and Sean fell to their knees and used their hands, working hard to expose the object.

Suddenly, they both jumped to their feet and moved back a few steps.

"Sweet Mother Mary," Connor slowly said.

"Shamrock . . . for . . . the . . . love . . . a . . . all that's holy," Sean whispered. They both blessed themselves and I quickly saw why—we had unearthed a metal coffin.

"Holy crap! Let's get it out of there," I said.

Shamrock and I knelt by the hole, using our hands to expose more of the coffin. Sean and Connor hesitated.

"Come on, lads," Shamrock said. "Don't be little girls. You both want to stay in America, right?"

The veiled threat seemed to work.

It took us the better part of an hour. Finally, with the help of the side handles on the casket, we were able to pull the casket free and set it on the sand. The two Irishmen looked at it so warily, I got the feeling they were waiting for the cover to open and its occupant to jump out.

"Look, Danny," Shamrock said, pointing to a silver plate on top of the casket.

I shined my flashlight on the plate.

Solomon Funeral Home, Roxbury, Mass.

Solomon. Albert Keel had mentioned a Boston gangster by the name, King Solomon. He'd been one of the smugglers. A front business? Maybe. Even so, it was ingenious to bury the gold in a metal coffin.

The four of us grabbed the side handles on the coffin and lifted. We headed back in the direction of my cottage. The coffin was so heavy, I knew I'd need more than a couple chiropractor visits to recover from this little adventure. We struggled as best we could, stopping occasionally to lower our burden to the sand and catch our breath.

"We need to fill in the hole so Dunn can't tell we've been digging here," I said to Shamrock. He immediately sent Conner and Sean back to do just that, then we resumed our trek.

After what was the longest hour of my life, we reached my cottage. I didn't think anyone had seen us. If they had, they'd likely wonder if they'd missed Halloween. Four men walking with a coffin between cottages—what a sight!

We capped off our efforts with Heinekens once we were safely inside.

"Let's toast to our discovery, my friends," Shamrock said, excitement glimmering in his eyes. "And another toast to Connor and Sean. My boys, just a friendly reminder that you don't speak to anyone about tonight."

"We'll never say a word," Connor said.

"My lips are sealed," Sean said.

Connor and Sean left for Irish Town without one question asked between them. The respect and influence Shamrock had with his countrymen was even more than I'd been aware of. I couldn't help wondering if his IRA background had a part to play in their high opinion of him.

After a few more celebratory beers, Shamrock and I dragged the coffin through the crawl-space door and into the middle area under my cottage.

Then I called Dianne and told her to come down and join us.

Chapter 36

DIANNE, SHAMROCK, AND I were sitting around, just starting to relax when feet pounding up my porch stairs shook the floor. I was glad my paranoia of recent events had caused me to lock the wood door, but that good feeling didn't last long.

The doorknob rattled, then there was a thunderous crash against the door and our favorite Irish thug, Cauliflower, aka Angus, burst into the room, stumbling to regain his balance and remain on his feet.

Butchy Dunn stomped through the door behind Angus. He looked none too happy. Angus gave me an icy stare and I noticed his hand was heavily bandaged from where I'd introduced it to a pencil point not too long ago.

Butchy gave each of us a threatening glare. "Okay assholes, I want it all . . . now. Where is it?"

No one answered.

"I guess you wanna end up like poor Monica?" he snarled.

"You filthy scum." Dianne spat, the first time I'd seen her do something like that. "Your own sister. You'll rot in hell, you bastard."

"You may be right, beautiful," Butchy grinned, "but imagine what I'll do to you three if I don't get it all . . . and now."

Dianne and Shamrock sat on the couch across from where I'd taken my normal seat in my easy chair. I could see the fear I felt reflected in both Dianne and Shamrock's terrified faces. Still, I wasn't about to hand over the gold to this low-life killer.

When none of us spoke, Butchy growled, "So . . . you wanna play it tough, huh? All of you?"

His face turned red as the sound of people talking came from outside.

"See who it is," Butchy said to Angus.

Angus stepped to the side windows, peeked through the blind slats, then said, "Christ, you gotta see this, Butchy. You won't believe it."

"Don't fuck around. What is it?"

"A bunch a local yokels," Angus said, "and they're carryin' shovels, metal detectors, and shit like that."

"I knew that dirty Hoar asshole couldn't keep his big trap shut," Butchy grumbled. "You probably figured that, too, huh, Marlowe? That's why I couldn't beat anything useful out of him. You kept him in the dark. When I see that scrawny little prick, I'm gonna smack him in the head with a shovel."

He glared down at my easy chair. "I guess it don't matter now if every dink on the beach comes down to play treasure hunt. We all know they're too late . . . right, Marlowe?"

He smacked the back of my chair with an open palm, making us all jump. "Where . . . is . . . it? I know you found it. I've been keeping an eye on you, Marlowe. Got hold of one a those Micks what helped you. He didn't last a minute before he told us everything. 'Course those cigarettes do kinda burn, so I can't really blame him. A fucking coffin! Who'd a thought? So . . . last time . . . where is it?"

Again, no one answered.

Butchy snarled. "I'm really losin' my patience here."

"Who cares?" I said.

"Still a wise ass, huh, Marlowe?" He hesitated for a second, then added, "Time to see just how tough you are, or if what I've heard about you from Hoar is all bullshit."

He pulled a rusty pair of pliers from the back pocket of his jeans. My heart skipped a beat and I wished I had a Xanax, maybe two.

"I always wanted to be a dentist." He nodded at Dianne. "I'm gonna start with your girl here, Marlowe. That way I won't be wastin' any time. Like I said, I'm losin' my patience."

He looked at Angus. "How many of her teeth do you think I can pull before he spills, Angus?"

Angus snickered. "Five."

"Nah. Don't believe the bullshit Hoar told us," Butchy said, shaking his head. "He won't make it past seein' one of her beautiful pearly whites being yanked."

Butchy took the rusty pliers, leaned over Dianne. Her lips became a thin, tight, white line and her eyes opened so wide I thought the corners would tear. Shamrock jumped off the couch and Angus pushed him right back down.

"Who's gonna be right, tough guy?" Butchy snarled at me. "Me or my associate here?"

"Neither," I said angrily, "because the only one around here who'll be needing dental work is you, Dunn."

The same paranoia that had caused me to lock the door had also influenced me to prop Betsy, my double-barrel shotgun, behind my easy chair. I reached around the back of my chair now, grabbed Betsy, and leveled her square at Butchy's chest. I cocked one barrel with a loud *click!*

Dianne and Shamrock both stood and moved as far from Butchy as they could. I was surprised Butchy didn't move to grab one or both of them.

"Take that thing away from him, Angus," Butchy said. "I'm gonna beat him to death with it."

Angus did an almost comical double take. I cocked the second barrel. The noise was just as intimidating as the first.

When Angus didn't move, Butchy screamed, "Whattaya waitin' for? Don't worry. He ain't got the balls."

And you know what? He was right. At least, I wouldn't have had the balls—except for the pictures running through my mind—images of Shamrock and Dianne dead, and maybe worse.

Sam was in those pictures, too. I knew Butchy wouldn't let the boy grow to manhood, give him a chance to find out what his uncle had done to his mother, and maybe take revenge some day.

Betsy felt good in my hands—pointed directly at Butchy Dunn, the worst of the worst.

Butchy must have sensed it, too. Realized he'd played his cards wrong. His eyes opened wide and he stepped back toward the window.

"No. Don't."

But the trigger pulled too damn easy. The roar of the gun didn't even bother me, although I noticed both Shamrock and Dianne jump.

Butchy was blown through the window. His body thudded on the porch outside.

Angus took one horrified look at me and the shotgun I'd turned in his direction. He held up both his hands, palms out. "Don't shoot. I don't give a shit about him or any of you. Just let me go. You'll never see me again." He was actually trembling.

I nodded.

Angus scrambled out the door and ran down the stairs and all the way to Charlestown from the sound of his feet beating it away.

Chapter 37

DUNN HAD ENDED up dead on my porch. Surprisingly enough, the cops—even my nemesis, Lieutenant Gant—had accepted our story. I had acted in self-defense. It helped that Dianne and Shamrock told the cops they both believed they were about to be killed by Butchy, who came to my cottage demanding money we didn't have.

To top it off, the cops realized that Dunn had most likely beaten Fred Capobianco to death.

A couple days later, the four of us—Dianne, Shamrock, James, and I—were at the Seashell outdoor concert venue across Ocean Boulevard from the Casino. It was a warm fall day with plenty of sun and the smell of salt in the air. Fortunately, the park service hadn't yet removed the wooden benches Seashell viewers used to watch the nightly summer music performers. We sat spread out on two back-to-back benches.

Inviting James had been my idea. Getting James involved could be a big plus in our current situation. He might have some good advice for us, considering what we were there to talk about. Not only had he been my occasional lawyer, he'd helped me out of a few beach scrapes I'd been involved with in the past. He wasn't above bending the law a bit to help his clients, although this time it hadn't been necessary.

"Tell you the truth, I don't think the cops were too upset to see Butchy taken off the chessboard," James said. "There was an officer from the Massachusetts Staties there, and Charlestown PD sent a captain to the station. The FBI even sent an agent. They all confirmed that Dunn was a stone-cold killer and a participant in every slimy racket in the Boston area. They did everything short of coming right out and saying they were glad Dunn was no more. So it looks like you slipped out of this one, too, Dan."

"What about the big Irish thug . . . Angus?" Shamrock asked. "What will he have to say?"

"He was no problem," James said. "There's a dozen outstanding felony warrants on him down in Mass., one for first-degree murder. No jury would have believed what he was saying, even if they'd listened to him."

"Thank god you're free, Dan," Dianne said.

That made me feel good and once again I wondered if our relationship could still be salvaged.

I'd told James most of our amazing story—even told him about the treasure—while sitting in his car outside the police station earlier. Later, he'd told me on the phone that he had some ideas. He'd given me the basics, but I was anxious to hear more.

Shamrock and Dianne knew James and seemed comfortable having him present. Even though I'd had to let one more person know of our secret, they both had agreed we would need legal advice. And who better than James?

I started the ball rolling. "We all know why we're here."

Shamrock nodded like an excited child. "Sure do . . . to figure out how we're going to divide the gold coins, Danny. I want to go home, see my ma." Without waiting for a response, he went on, "There's four of us, so let's divide the coins in four shares and be done with it."

We had already agreed that Sam would get Monica's share. That was another reason I'd invited James—to make sure we did right by the boy. If we screwed up our windfall, that was one thing, but I didn't want to jeopardize the boy's future.

"There's twelve hundred and fifty coins to share," Dianne said. "So wouldn't it be best to give each of us 312 coins? Add in the extra half? If they're worth at least a thousand each, as you said, Dan, that's $312,500 each."

Dianne was a good businesswoman and I didn't doubt she was running all these calculations in her head.

I pointed at my attorney sitting on the bench in front of me. "That's why I suggested James. He can explain some things. You both know him and know how well he's treated me in the past."

"Go ahead then, James," Dianne said. "Talk to us."

"First of all," James began, "together you have over a thousand very rare and expensive gold coins. You can't start running around willy-nilly trying to sell them to coin dealers. They'd notify the cops so fast your heads would spin."

"I'll sell mine in Boston and after I go see my mother, I'll get me one of those little two-seater Mercedes convertible jobs. Always liked those suckers," Shamrock said, his ruddy face beaming.

"You can't do that, Shamrock. James just said you can't sell them in Boston," Dianne said.

"Why not?" Shamrock asked. He bounced on the bench, the metal legs clacking against the cement as he did. "It's my money, isn't it?"

"Yes," James said again. "But if you did that—sell the coins in Boston—the feds . . . the IRS . . . would be all over you like a cheap suit. Believe me, they'd be on all of you before the next high tide. They're good at what they do."

Shamrock intensified his bouncing. "How do we get our money then?"

My next idea might go over like a lead balloon, although I really wasn't sure what to expect. "I was wondering about Sam, Monica's son. You've all met him. Know what a great kid he is. And we all want to remember Monica's wishes for him."

"Yeah," Shamrock said. "Yes, we do. Don't worry, Danny, the boy will get his mom's share. We already decided that."

"I was wondering what everyone would think of giving a little part of our shares so Sam's aunt could get a house in the suburbs, get Sam out of the projects. That was Monica's dream. And without her, none of us would have anything."

"That's true, Danny," Shamrock said. "Without Monica we would never have heard of the treasure."

Dianne furrowed her brows and looked directly at me. "Isn't her share enough for that?"

"Not really," James said, "especially at the slow pace we're going to have to work this. That is, if you all agree with what I'm going to propose."

"Slow pace!" Shamrock exclaimed. "What do you mean, slow pace? I don't like the sound of that one bit."

"Look, Shamrock." James sighed. "You can't go around to coin stores selling expensive and extremely rare coins all over New England. Rare coin dealing is a very close, tight-knit community and they rarely ever see even one of these coins. If you all start dumping them, even just one or two at a time, every coin dealer on the east coast will know some-one is unloading a bunch of special coins. They'll be suspi-cious and the feds will find out—all it takes is one phone call from a suspicious dealer. Feds'll be on your trail that very day, believe me. Before long, they'll trace a coin back to one of you and then they'll figure out who the others are. After that, they'll use surveillance, tax audits, and other nasty tricks—for years if need be—until they confiscate all the coins and anything else of value they can seize from you, using unpaid taxes as the excuse. And that'll be the end of that."

"Well, what's your proposal, then?" Dianne asked.

"As I said," James continued, "you aren't going to be able to sell many, if any, of the coins without raising a ton of red flags. On the other hand, I have an acquaintance who can con-vert the coins to cash for you without attracting attention."

"If we can't do it, how is that possible?" Dianne asked.

"All I can tell you," James said, "is that none of these coins will ever be seen in the United States again."

"I get it," Shamrock said. "This guy'll dump them in an-other country to dealers or collectors where no American cops will be nosing around. Good idea. But . . . what about that slow pace you're talking about?"

"I already told Dan." James rubbed his hands on his thighs. "This guy can only move so many at a time over there. There may be one decent chunk of dough for each of you the first time, then after that we'll have to pace the distribu-tion out slowly. After that first amount, you'll all be getting maybe a couple grand every month or so."

Shamrock and Dianne sighed in unison.

"I know it's not what we were hoping for," I added, "but James assures me that his connection is the best and will get us the highest prices possible for the coins and that eventually we'll be paid for all of them. He swears we'll be paid for everything. And I believe him."

"Shamrock?" James asked.

"If it sounds okay to Danny, then I'm in."

"Dianne?" I asked.

"Under one condition," she replied.

"What's that?" I asked, dreading what I might hear.

Dianne looked at me with those gorgeous green eyes. "You promise to get rid of that shit box of yours and get a better car?" she said with a straight face.

That was an almost pleasant surprise. "I thought you liked my little green Chevette."

Dianne covered her eyes with her hand. "I hate that thing. It's mortifying. If I have to ride down Ocean Boulevard in it once more, I'll jump out."

"I agree," Shamrock said. "I hate to say it, Danny, but it is a crate. Probably dangerous, too. You deserve something a little classier."

I couldn't deny that. "You never complained when I gave you those rides to the girlie joints over in Seabrook."

"Don't get your knickers in a twist," Shamrock grinned. "I just meant you should have something a little nicer and safer. And let's not talk about those couple of wayward times."

I guffawed. "A couple? Okay . . . if you want to call it a couple, then a couple it is."

"Any charge for this, James?" Dianne asked.

Like I said, Dianne is good with business.

"Only fifteen percent," James answered.

Dianne's calculator mind must have been crunching the numbers. "That sounds like a lot."

"Not really. My contact will take care of my fee which isn't much, believe me," James said. "If this was hot stuff and you were dealing with a fence, he'd want half. This is a lot safer. You'll get the best price for those coins and no one's going to get ripped off. You'll each get every penny you've got coming. My word on that. I've worked with this person many times . . . he's the best. You have no worries, I promise."

Dianne looked at me. So did Shamrock. After all, I'd had some experience with such things in the past.

"Sounds fine," I said. "I think James has got a great outlet for the coins. I think we're lucky, seeing we don't have any alternatives."

"Okay," she said, "let's do it."

"This is slowly getting chipped away at," Shamrock said.

"We still have plenty," I offered. "After Eddie's two hundred bucks, the rest is ours."

"We really have to pay that sleazebag, Danny?" Shamrock asked with a scowl.

"We have to make sure he keeps his mouth shut," I said. "Not that he needs an excuse to flap his gums, but I'm not going to give him one. And it's only two hundred. That's cheap to get rid of him."

"You're right about that," Shamrock said with a smile.

"Speaking of waste products, I have good news," James said. "Hoar and Doller both violated parole and, best I can make out, they may be doing a couple years each. So they won't be around the beach to mouth off anyway. And judging by what you told me, Dan, they don't know any specifics. If they start talking about gold, the cops will just chalk it up to one of Hoar's pipe dreams. They know he's a con man."

"Now that's great news—Eddie in jail." Shamrock beamed. "So, when do we get that first big payment you mentioned, counselor?"

"A few weeks, tops," James said. "But remember, it's not going to be gigantic. We have to do this right. It'll be substantial and you'll all be happy. In the end, you will get everything—"

"What else?" Dianne asked, apparently picking up that James was holding back something. When James didn't answer, she continued, "I know you and Dan want to talk about Sam, so go ahead."

"To get back to what Dan started to say a few minutes ago," James said. "I propose to help the boy. Well, this is really Dan's proposal . . . that all three of you give up your odd twelve coins each. That'll still leave you three hundred coins apiece, and that extra thirty-six for the boy should total at least $36,000 or so. I'll set up a trust for him and only for him. With Monica's first payout and what you three have offered, if you agree, I'll be able to set up a sufficiently funded real estate trust to get a decent house in the suburbs for him and his aunt, without raising suspicion. We might even be able to partially fund his college in the future."

There were smiles all round.

"What do you all say?" I looked at Shamrock first.

"Let's go for it," he answered. "I still have three hundred rare coins. That's more than I ever thought I'd have."

"Dianne?" I asked, looking at her dark hair blowing in the ocean breeze.

"Of course," she replied. "I wouldn't want anyone, especially that sweet boy, ending up like his uncle Butchy."

James rubbed his nose with the back of his hand. No sniffing today though. I was happy about that. He must have thought this was serious enough a situation to abstain for a day.

There was one thing I wanted to mention, but I was very apprehensive about it. I'd hoped to get Dianne by herself to discuss it, but the way things were between us, I had no idea when that might be. Dianne's answer to my question might have a bearing on how the cash dispersal would be done.

So I pulled up my big boy pants and turned to Dianne. "Would you ever consider having someone buy into the Tide as a full partner?"

Both Shamrock and James looked away, pretending not to hear, although I knew they were as anxious as I was to hear Dianne's answer.

"Who would the someone be?" Dianne asked. "Is he reliable?"

"He used to be," I answered. "And he's going to be again. For good this time. He promises." And I meant it.

Dianne reached across the bench and took my hand in hers. "There isn't enough room on the sign to add my name, anyway. So I guess we'll have to keep it Dan Marlowe's High Tide Restaurant and Saloon." She squeezed my hand. "Does that answer your question?"

I squeezed right back.

Funny how even the unluckiest people hit once in a while.

Shamrock and James were both smiling. The sun shone on their faces as it dropped behind the Casino building across the street from us.

Was there any better place to be in this crazy, mixed-up world than Hampton Beach, sitting on a bench with someone I was hoping might be my girl again—and my friends? To top it off, I'd soon be the proud half owner of the best restaurant and bar within miles. If there was something better than all that, I couldn't imagine what it could be.

James stood and headed for his crate of a car parked illegally at the curb. His battered brown briefcase swung by his side as he walked around to the driver's door and got in.

"I'll be in touch soon," he called.

The three of us watched as he drove off.

I wondered if Dianne and Shamrock felt like I did— that I had won the lottery. My friends deserved it. That must mean I deserved it, too.

We said our goodbyes and went our separate ways.

On the walk home, I wondered what kind of car I'd get to fulfill my promise to Dianne . . . after I took care of my kids and made arrangements with my ex-wife so they could visit their dad at the beach again. A father who was fully rehabilitated, a successful business owner, and actually flush for a change.

I prayed it would last and swore to myself I would make sure that it did: The "new and improved Dan Marlowe"— complete with a lifetime guarantee.

Let's all keep our fingers crossed.

About the Author

JED POWER is a Hampton Beach, NH-based writer and author of numerous published short stories. *The Boss of Hampton Beach*, *Hampton Beach Homicide*, *Blood on Hampton Beach*, *Honeymoon Hotel*, *Murder on the Island*, *The Hampton Beach Tapes*, and *Hampton Beach Heist* are the seven previous novels in the Dan Marlowe/Hampton Beach, NH, crime series.

The Combat Zone, the first crime novel in a planned new series, is out now. The novel follows a P.I. who hangs his hat in early 1970s Harvard Square and roams the Combat Zone, Boston's notorious red-light district. This novel was a finalist in the St. Martin's Press/Private Eye Writers of America "Best First P.I. Novel" competition.

All books are available in both paper and ebook.

Find out more at www.darkjettypublishing.com